Desperately Seeking Fireman

Also by Jennifer Bernard

Desperately Seeking Fireman

A BACHELOR FIREMEN NOVELLA

JENNIFER BERNARD

AVONIMPULSE
An Imprint of HarperCollinsPublishers

Excerpt from *Four Weddings and a Fireman* copyright © 2013 by Jennifer Bernard.

Excerpt from *Once Upon a Highland Summer* copyright © 2013 by Lecia Cotton Cornwall.

Excerpt from *Hard Target* copyright © 2013 by Kay Thomas.

Excerpt from *The Wedding Date* copyright © 2013 by Lisa Connelly.

Excerpt from *Torn* copyright © 2013 by Karen Erickson.

Excerpt from *The Cupcake Diaries: Spoonful of Christmas* copyright © 2013 by Darlene Panzera.

Excerpt from *Rodeo Queen* copyright © 2013 by Tina Klinesmith.

EPub Edition JANUARY 2014 ISBN: 9780062329561

Print Edition ISBN: 9780062329578

JV 10 9 8 7 6 5 4 3 2 1

Chapter One

Wayside Chapel, San Gabriel, California

THE GROOM'S SIDE of the aisle was packed with an astonishingly high number of gorgeous men. Nita Moreno, standing near Melissa McGuire, soon to be Brody, surveyed the pews with widening eyes. There was enough testosterone in the building to fuel a small nation's army—enough handsome, manly faces to fill an issue of *Playgirl* and enough brawny muscles to—

Oops. Busted. From across the aisle, two steps behind Captain Brody, a pair of amused, tiger-striped eyes met hers. An unusual mixture of gold and green, surrounded by thick black eyelashes, they would have made their owner look feminine if he weren't one solid hunk of hard-packed male. A smile twitched at the corner of his mouth. Even in this context, the so-called Bachelor Firemen crowding the wedding of their revered fire captain, he stood out. First there was that breath-taking physique. Then there was his face, a study in contrasts. His features were so strong they almost qualified as harsh. Firm jaw, uncompromising cheekbones. A man's man, until one looked into those golden eyes, or noticed that he possessed the most beautiful mouth Nita had ever seen on a man.

She narrowed her own eyes and met him look for look. Hey, she wasn't checking out the available men. She had one of her own. Very deliberately, she let her gaze roam to the bride's side of the aisle and settle on Bradford Maddox IV. Hedge fund operator, family scion, possessor of a killer business instinct and only a slightly receding hairline, he was hers, and she could still scarcely believe it. Maybe soon she and Bradford would be making their way down an aisle like this. Out of unconscious nervous habit, she clamped down on the inside of her cheek with her teeth. She loved Bradford, and knew he felt the same. He must.

Bradford, who seemed lost in thought, startled when he realized she was looking adoringly at him. He gave her a faint smile, then pressed his finger to his ear. Lovely. He wasn't lost in thought, he was listening to his Bluetooth. She sighed, telling herself to let it go. It came with the territory when you dated a hotshot financier. Of course he couldn't focus his *entire* attention on the wedding of two people he didn't even know.

The right side of her body felt suddenly warm, and she realized the man across the aisle was still watching her, as if she fascinated him.

Really? *She* fascinated *him*? That seemed unlikely. She raised a questioning eyebrow at him. He smiled, the expression transforming his face from the inside out. Goodness, the man was gorgeous, in a totally different way from Bradford. Dark instead of blond, tough instead of charming, virile and primitive—the kind of man who would toss you over his shoulder and have his way with you.

He jerked his chin at her, as if signaling her to meet him in the chancel.

She frowned at him, scolding. *Excuse me? How inappropriate.*

He did it again, more urgently this time.

What did the man want? She lifted her hands, palms up, in a frustrated question, as he mouthed something to her.

"Bouquet."

Aw, crap. She swiveled toward Melissa, who had twisted in her direction, unholy mirth lighting up her forest-green eyes. The ivory antique lace adorning her bodice quivered as she held in her laughter.

The first glitch, after Nita had worked so hard to plan her friend's wedding to perfection.

Digging deep for solemn dignity, Nita stepped forward and received the bride's bouquet so that Melissa could marry her fire captain. She stepped back into position, fixing her gaze on the delicate ruffles of the white peonies, their petals as fine as living parchment, their fresh scent soothing the edge from her embarrassment. Gnawing at the inside of her cheek helped too.

As soon as the reception started, she was going to throttle that man, whoever he was. In the meantime, there was a little thing called a wedding underway.

"I will," said Captain Brody, slipping a simple gold ring on Melissa's finger and radiating a passionate devotion that made tears spring to Nita's eyes.

"And will you, Melissa Eleanor McGuire, take this man to have and to hold, to care for and to cherish, for the rest of your days?"

"I will."

The deep joy in her friend's voice propelled one of those tears down Nita's cheek. It landed on a peony petal, where it left a translucent smudge.

She blinked madly, refusing to draw any more attention away from Melissa. If someone was going to cry, it ought to be the bride, not the bridesmaid. Or maybe it ought to be the man across the aisle. Daring to raise her eyes again, she saw that he was once again staring directly at her. This time he didn't look so much amused as . . . well, enchanted. Intrigued. *Attracted.* A bolt of heat traveled from the crown of her head all the way to the soles of her feet.

For a crazy moment, she wondered if she'd been struck by lightning for ogling a man during her dearest friend's wedding.

San Gabriel Inn—private dining room

MAKE THAT, OGLING a *married* man during her friend's wedding. A married man with a bubbly, blond wife and a willowy teenage daughter. The three of them sat at a round table across the room. His arm was slung across the back of his wife's chair as she chatted with the woman next to her, who Nita recognized as Sabina Jones, one of San Gabriel's female firefighters. The man himself was laughing with his daughter, whose dark hair was fastened at her neck with a flower-clip. The deep rumble of his laugh made its way across the room to her, even through the animated chatter of wedding guests.

Altogether, they made a perfect picture of a happy family. They made her teeth ache. Or maybe some other part of her body ached; she didn't care to investigate.

Standing at the bar as Bradford continued the phone conversation he'd begun during the ceremony, Nita pressed his arm against her side, as if to remind herself of her good fortune. Bradford—he hated being called Brad—had chosen *her*. A supporter of her boss Senator Stryker, he was perfect for her in every way. Both driven and hard-working, they had similar goals. Both wanted to be the best at what they did. Both wanted to make their mark on the world. They understood each other and respected each other. She was lucky, lucky, lucky. And she loved him.

An image of Melissa's peonies fluttered through her mind. Funny how flowers didn't have to work so hard to be perfect. They just *were*. Imagine if flowers had to put in late nights to get ahead. Imagine if flowers had to worry about appropriate hairstyles and trends in business attire. The whimsical thought made her smile.

"A glass of champagne for your thoughts," said a deep

voice in her ear. She swung around, somehow knowing instantly to whom the voice belonged. For safety, she kept her hand nestled snugly in the crook of Bradford's arm.

Wise move. As she met the man's tiger eyes, awareness flashed across her every nerve ending.

"No, thank you. I'm with someone," she said, which immediately sounded not only like a non sequitur, but completely obvious since she was smushed up against Bradford.

"Does he know that?" The man's raised eyebrow indicated the phone conversation in which Bradford was still immersed.

"Of course he knows. He's a very busy, important man, that's all. He's working on a million-dollar deal. Billion-dollar, I mean."

"You're sure it isn't a kajillion dollar deal?" Again, with that amusement. He was *teasing* her. Which was really only one step removed from flirting if you thought about it. How dare he flirt with her while his bubbly, pretty wife was sitting right over there?

Nita decided to go on the offensive. "Beautiful wedding, wasn't it? Wedding vows are so important, don't you think?"

His face immediately went shuttered, as if all the light had been snuffed out. "I do," he murmured. "You have no idea how much." He turned away from her and signaled to the bartender, while she turned that cryptic statement over in her mind.

He ordered a Dos Equis and a glass of sparkling wine, then launched into a conversation with the bartender about the baseball playoffs. On her other side, Bradford was saying something about "debt burden" and "leverage." Neither conversation held a candle to the speculation cartwheeling through her brain. When the baseball conversation paused so the bartender could do his job, she tapped the man on the arm. God, it was like a rock. Barely any give at all beneath her fingertips.

"Excuse me, but I was wondering what you meant by that," she asked when he turned back to her.

"You ever been married?"

"No. Not yet," she added defensively. Ask her again in six months, and she hoped to have a different answer.

"Then you wouldn't understand." With that dismissive remark, he collected his drinks, left an oversized tip on the bar—Bradford would be shocked—and wound his way through the crowd to his table. She felt annoyed with herself for assuming the man had been flirting with her simply because she found him so attractive.

"How irritating," she said to no one in particular. Except that Melissa had materialized at her side.

"No one's allowed to be irritated at my wedding," she told Nita.

"Sorry. Maybe you shouldn't have invited *him*." She gestured toward the broad, receding back of the mystery man. "Whoever he is."

"That's Jeb Stone, captain of the C shift."

"I don't know what that means, but I take it he, too, is a San Gabriel firefighter?" Melissa had been Nita's closest friend in Los Angeles before moving home to San Gabriel, meeting Captain Harry Brody and falling head over heels in love. Melissa was a TV news producer; Nita, as State Senator Stryker's press secretary, had fed her plenty of scoops over the years.

"Yes, he's a captain just like Brody." Melissa's face lit with tenderness as she said her new husband's name. "Brody's favorite captain, but don't tell anyone else that."

"I thought they were all supposed to be *Bachelor* Firemen. Isn't he married?" Okay, so some part of her was hoping against hope that he wasn't married, that he was attending the wedding with his sister or the station receptionist who needed a date.

"The stories are exaggerated. Some of them are married. Jeb is, Double D is," she indicated a big-bellied man towing his wife to the dance floor, "but most are not. Vader's single." She pointed to a younger guy with a world-class body-builder physique then continued on a dizzyingly fast tour of the men present. "Stud," an eager, brown-haired cutie, "Psycho," electric blue eyes and edgy bad-boy vibe, "Hoagie," handsome heartbreaker-type, "and that's just the A shift. B and C are another story. I don't know them as well. But I think the ratio of single to married is pretty consistent."

Nita wasn't interested in the ratio of anything except Jeb Stone's broad shoulders to his lean hips.

And that of his ring finger to the rest of his digits.

Her attention had snagged on the words, "Jeb is," and stayed there. Jeb is married. Jeb is taken. Jeb is not for you. *What did it matter anyway?* She chewed at the inside of her mouth. Bradford was the man for her.

Just then Bradford finished his call and bent his charming, social register countenance on Melissa. "Lovely wedding. I'm honored by the invitation."

From Melissa's curl of a smile, Nita could tell she didn't like Bradford. "Thank you so much for coming. Nita is one of my favorite people in the world, and she did an amazing job helping me plan. I'm so glad you could both be here."

Yep, definitely didn't like him.

"Here's hoping that the next time we're all at a wedding, someone else is saying those vows." He transferred his smile to Nita, who took a moment to put his meaning together. When she did, a soaring giddiness nearly overwhelmed her. Bradford *was* thinking marriage. What else could he have meant? Bradford Maddox IV was considering marriage to *her*. This wasn't a one-sided love, the way part of her kept fearing.

So there, Mr. Non-Bachelor Fireman.

She shot one last glance at Jeb Stone, who had risen to his feet and was taking his wife's hand in his. With a wry expression, his wife said something out of the side of her mouth, something intended just for him. He responded with an intimate chuckle. They were perfect together. Revoltingly perfect.

Wrenching her gaze back to her own date, she kissed her future husband on the cheek. She and Bradford were just as perfect together as Jeb and his wife were. See if they weren't.

Chapter Two

Three years later

JEB STONE CRUISED along the Pacific Coast Highway in his rented Maserati, which he'd nicknamed Ira because it cost more than his retirement fund. A whiff of coconut caught his attention, followed by a cascade of giggles delivered by a Porsche full of blondes as they whizzed past him. They laughed and shook out their long hair, waving at him with gratifying flirtatiousness. The sultry driver winked, and another girl ran her tongue over her lips, porno-style, as she stared at him invitingly.

He suppressed the urge to inform them that they were going fifteen miles per hour over the speed limit and that cutting accident victims out of mangled wrecks was one of the worst jobs a firefighter faced.

Instead he gave them a brief smile from behind his sunglasses. Let them hang on to their illusion that he was some Malibu millionaire. Let them think he drove a Maserati every day, instead of the ten-year-old truck he'd inherited in the divorce. Let them think he was on his way to a meeting with Steven Spielberg, instead of . . . well, nowhere in particular. Just going. Away. Alone. For the first time in eighteen years.

His phone rang, which made him jump because it was plugged into the sound system of the sports car. He pressed the button the rental clerk had showed him. It had taken the guy half an hour to walk him through the car's many life-altering features.

"Hey, Daddy-o." Alison's chipper voice boomed from the speakers. He turned the volume down so the rest of Malibu, and maybe even the ships at sea, couldn't hear his daughter.

"Hi sweetie. How's Thailand?"

This was code for "how's your mother." As planned, his ex-wife Belinda had filed for divorce a week after Alison had turned eighteen. The next day, she'd gotten on a plane to Thailand, where she'd booked herself a two-week yoga retreat.

A year later, Alison had gone to check on her. "Better than I expected," she said now. "Very happy. Weirdly happy."

Jeb felt the familiar boulder-sized weight in his heart ease just a bit. It was about time Belinda was happy. They'd met young, gotten pregnant by accident and married, but they'd never made each other particularly happy, for reasons that now seemed obvious. The sex part of the marriage had ended four years before the rest of it.

But at least Alison had turned out great. He pictured her in his mind's eye, so tall and confident. With her dark hair and hazel eyes, Alison looked a lot like him, if she were a workaholic, jaded fireman.

"I'm glad she's happy. Really glad."

"Now it's your turn, Daddy-o. I'm serious. I want both my parents smiling."

"Oh no. No more dates. No more Match.com, no more of your Zumba teachers. I'm driving an Italian sports car next to the Pacific Ocean on a gorgeous day, talking to my gorgeous daughter. What could be better?"

"You're about to find out. I made an offering for you at a temple here. And I got Mom's whole yoga class to chant a love prayer. You're going down, Dad. Down like a broken elevator. Down like Bieber's career."

"That college is worth every penny."

"Don't change the subject. I'm just calling to warn you, that's all. You're going down like —"

"You don't know who you're dealing with here, missy. I have immunity."

"If you're talking about the Bachelor Firemen curse, not to worry. I dedicated a prayer flag to breaking that silly thing, if it even exists."

"Oh, it exists all right—" Another call flashed on the screen, this one from the firehouse. "I'd better go," he told Alison. "Lay off the prayers and focus on the pad thai, okay? I love you."

"Love you too. But you're going down like a turkey on Thanksgiving—"

"Stone," he answered the incoming call.

"It's Brody." Captain Brody was captain of the A shift, and a legend in San Gabriel. As a captain himself, Jeb could connect with Brody in a way he couldn't with the other firefighters. Just from the sound of his voice, he knew something was wrong.

"I need a huge favor," said Brody.

"Done. But I'm on vacation. I'm driving up the coast."

"I know. That's why I'm calling. Melissa got a tip on a hot story and up and left. Eight months pregnant and she decides it's a good idea to get on a boat to track down some senator. A boat. In the ocean. Eight months."

"Senator Stryker?" The man had been on the front page of every paper the last couple of days. Some scandal or other. Jeb hadn't bothered to read the stories.

"Maybe. I don't care if it's the President of Mars, she shouldn't be risking the baby."

"What do you want me to do?" Jeb knew Melissa well enough to know she was intelligent, independent, and not at all reckless.

"She's headed to Santa Lucia Island. That's where the senator's hiding out, though if you tell any other member of the press she might divorce me."

Jeb also knew both Brody and Melissa well enough to know that wasn't going to happen. They were madly in love—real love, the kind he and Belinda had never quite managed.

Brody continued. "Santa Lucia is right off the coast. The ferries go twice a day. I'd go but I'm shorthanded here and can't leave. Besides, Melissa would kill me. All I want you to do is go out there and keep an eye on her.

You can say it's a coincidence. You're on vacation. Lots of people go to San-L for vacation. She won't suspect a thing."

Jeb had a sinking feeling that wasn't likely. Melissa was no dummy. But no matter what, he couldn't turn down his fellow captain. Especially when the man sounded desperate enough to call out the Coast Guard. What the hell, he wasn't going anywhere in particular. Why not an island somewhere in that sparkly blue carpet of ocean to his left?

"Sure, Brody. I'll stalk your wife and unborn baby for you. What are friends for?"

Brody let out an unwilling laugh. "Nothing surreptitious that'll set off her alarm bells. You're just enjoying a coincidental vacation in the same place she is."

"Coincidental vacation. Got it."

"Call me as often as you can. I owe you, Stone."

"It's not a problem, Brody. Now try to relax. Have you been practicing your breathing?"

Jeb savored the long moment of silence that followed. Brody might intimidate the other guys, but not him. Besides, he'd been through that particular rodeo before. Nothing, not even breathing practice, could really prepare you.

"Yes," Brody finally said in a strangled sort of voice. "Vader's been working with me on it."

Jeb let out a belly laugh at the thought of the big muscleman Vader Brown training Brody on breathing techniques. "Good man. Hang in there, tough guy. Everything's going to be fine."

Finding the PCH momentarily empty in both directions, he swung the Maserati around in the sort of tight turn the thing was probably designed for. Of course, most drivers weren't heading after another man's very pregnant wife in pursuit of a scandal-ridden senator in hiding. But what else were vacations for?

So far, nothing on this trip had chased away the hollow feeling he'd been experiencing ever since both Belinda and Alison had left San Gabriel. No matter how many dates he went on, how many extra duties he assumed at the station, life felt off-kilter. He'd been a family man for so long, even if that family had some unusual quirks. Alone, nothing felt quite right. Even this "vacation" felt strange.

Truthfully, it was a relief to have something useful to do.

ON SANTA LUCIA Island's ferry landing, Nita shaded her eyes against the myriad crystal reflections shimmering off the turquoise waves of the Pacific Ocean. How she'd managed to leave her sunglasses behind was a mystery, though perhaps explained by the fact that Senator Stryker had woken her at three in the morning and given her ten minutes to pack. And that was on top of three sleepless nights working to contain the world's most ridiculous scandal. And *that* was on top of nearly a year of numb misery during which she'd virtually sleepwalked through her days.

She nibbled at the inside of her cheek, a habit that had

gotten worse over the past horrible year. Press secretaries dealt with all sorts of unwelcome media attention, but not many had to explain that their boss had a secret drag queen identity who liked to post selfies of himself in body-shaping underwear and lots of makeup. "Senator Spanx" was now the hottest trending topic on every social media outlet.

When all hell had broken loose, everyone else had abandoned the senator. His wife and family were furious. Only Nita had been too numb to object when Stryker had dragged her to Santa Lucia. After a week holed up at the Enchanted Garden Inn, assessing the public's reaction to his embarrassing but ultimately harmless secret, she'd convinced him to give an exclusive interview to the only reporter he trusted, Melissa McGuire.

The ferry, which the locals called the *Danny B.*, churned toward the island. She had to admit, there were worse places the senator could have picked. Most of Santa Lucia was a nature preserve, with only a few hiking trails and bird-watching spots. The little town of Santa Lucia consisted of a tidy collection of pastel-painted homes, cute as eggs in an Easter basket, and a few municipal buildings such as the Town Hall and the volunteer fire department. The place had more charm than Candyland. But Nita knew it also had a serious side, hardy fishermen who braved all kinds of weather. Angie, the elderly owner of the Enchanted Garden, had told her that winter storms could leave the island cut off for weeks.

The usual chaotic crowd milled around on the weathered planks of the landing. Year-round residents waited to pick up groceries or visitors. Tourists snapped pictures or held up their iPads to record the adorableness, as if Santa Lucia were a new puppy.

The *Danny B.* drew closer, rocking from side to side on the ocean swells. Nita felt her anticipation mount. Even in the midst of a crisis, she couldn't wait to see Melissa. She hadn't seen her friend since the wedding. It had been a while since they'd even talked on the phone, maybe as long as a year. All the ups and downs with Bradford had consumed her, and she'd let their friendship slide. During the past nightmare of a year, she'd barely talked to any of her friends.

She scanned the passengers crowding the railing of the *Danny B.*, searching for Melissa's chocolate-brown hair and green eyes, but the only woman with brown hair was hugely pregnant, about to pop, it seemed, and that couldn't possibly be—

"Melissa?"

"Nita!" Melissa waved madly from the boat. "I made it!"

Nita couldn't answer through the sudden onrush of stupid pain. She fought it back. *This is Melissa. You love Melissa. Melissa will be a great mom.*

After the ferry tied off at the dock and the deckhands lowered the ramp, the passengers traipsed off, one by one. As soon as Melissa set foot on the dock, she dropped her overnight bag and waddled toward Nita.

"You're *pregnant*," said Nita, hugging her as hard as she dared.

"That's so rude. What if I'd just gained a little weight?" Melissa's beaming grin took the sting out of her words.

"I'm so excited for you!" If it sounded a little forced, who could blame her? The sentiment truly was sincere. "But why didn't you tell me? When's the baby due?"

"I didn't tell you because . . . well, you hadn't been returning my calls lately. And when you finally called me, I was afraid you'd talk me out of coming. And I'm already getting enough heat about this trip." With that, Melissa turned and aimed a deadly glare toward the boat ramp.

Nita followed her glance and got the shock of a lifetime. Six feet of stunning man stood with his feet braced apart, his arms folded over his broad chest, watching her with an impassive expression. Dark hair, eyes hidden behind sunglasses, the most beautiful mouth she'd ever seen on a man. A light layer of stubble set it off, as did the black leather jacket he was wearing. She knew that mouth. In three years, she'd never quite forgotten it.

Jeb Stone.

"What's . . . I'm confused. What's *he* doing here?"

"Brody took it upon himself to set a guard dog on me. I mean, seriously, doesn't he know that women used to work in the fields until they gave birth? Then slip that baby in a sling and keep on working? I have a brain, Nita." Melissa tapped her temple. "It still works even though my belly is as big as that ferryboat." Nita felt a tingle of anxiety. Melissa had always been calm and collected. She couldn't remember her ever sounding on the edge of hysteria like this.

"So he followed you here?"

"Yes. It's outrageous. I don't need a babysitter and

Brody ought to know that. How am I supposed to work with that . . . guard dog breathing down my neck?"

Jeb was looking rather Rottweiler-like, as if he were ready to pounce.

"It's sweet that Brody's so worried," Nita ventured.

"Sweet? It's bossy. If he had his way, I'd spend the next month in bed while he massaged my feet."

"That's . . . terrible?" Nita wasn't sure of the right response, since Bradford had never once offered her a foot massage.

"These firemen are impossible." Melissa raised her voice so Jeb couldn't avoid hearing her. "They're over-protective, macho, bossy, and they don't know when to back off."

Jeb grabbed Melissa's overnight bag, which she'd dropped near the foot of the ramp, and strode forward. "I'd like to book a room in the same place Melissa's staying."

Nita looked at Melissa, who shook her head violently. "You absolutely cannot give him a room."

"I don't own the place," Nita said carefully. "It's not really up to me."

"But the senator booked the whole inn, right?" Melissa said. "I told Jeb there wouldn't be room for him."

Jeb whipped off his sunglasses, the movement screaming of irritation. *Those eyes.* Tiger stripes, burning bright. "Can I speak to you in private for a moment?" he asked Nita.

Melissa's lips tightened, but just then her phone rang. Rolling her eyes, she answered it. Before Nita could quite realize what was happening, a strong hand gripped her upper arm and led her away from Melissa's vicinity. At his touch, Nita's heart started up a game of hopscotch in her chest.

Facing each other, she noticed he looked older, as if the last three years had taken a toll. She probably looked much the same.

"I think it's pretty clear that Melissa isn't entirely herself," he said in a low voice. "She needs me, whether she admits it or not. Can I count on you to help me out here?"

"I don't know. She seems pretty opposed to having you around."

"No kidding. What tipped you off?"

Her temper flared. "Hey, don't get sarcastic with me. I'm an innocent bystander here."

"Yeah? The way she tells it, you called her and begged her to come. Do you really think eight months pregnant is the right time to be traveling this far out to sea?"

Never mind that she hadn't known Melissa was pregnant. Did the man have to be so condescending? She folded her arms across her chest. "I'm starting to see why she's annoyed. And I still don't see why she'd need *you* around. Your manners are horrible. You didn't even say hello to me."

His head jerked back a bit. He frowned at her. She noticed lines fanning from the corners of his gold-striped eyes. "I wasn't sure you remembered me."

Was he kidding? He wasn't the sort of man you forgot. Not if you were a woman.

"Hello," he added, almost as an afterthought. Then

smiled. And oh God, that smile seemed to work its way from the core of his being, outward to his beautiful mouth, with its full lower lip and sensual upper lip. Killer smile. Killer everything. "It's nice to see you again."

The rote words reminded her that he was married and had the perfect family. "Likewise." Which wasn't exactly true, but oddly, wasn't exactly untrue, either.

"How've you been? How's Mr. Million Dollar Deal?"

A slow wave of heat traveled through her. He really *did* remember. "Gone. How are your marriage vows?"

"Voided by mutual agreement."

Well. *Well.*

Suddenly she felt so lightheaded she couldn't think of a thing to say. She cleared her throat. He leaned toward her ever so slightly. She felt as if she was standing on a ship that was rocking back and forth.

Just then Melissa marched toward them. "I promised Brody I wouldn't use my big belly to push Jeb off the dock. But that doesn't mean I'm cool with this whole thing. Anyway, how about we figure this situation out somewhere with a bathroom?"

Chapter Three

OF ALL THE luck. Jeb couldn't believe Nita Moreno, the same woman he'd nearly made an ass of himself over at Brody's wedding, had turned up again. He remembered being unable to stop staring at her, drawn by the dark satin of her hair piled in glossy, tumbling curls. The wild rose color of her bridesmaid's dress had made her skin glow like sunlit honey. She looked thinner now, in a way that suggested she'd been sick. But she still wore that confident poise that both drew him and made him want to get under her skin.

Just before Brody's wedding, Belinda had told him that she wanted an open relationship, and that he was free to pursue someone else. When he laid eyes on Nita Moreno, he'd been tempted. Extremely tempted. Until she'd shot him down with her billionaire boyfriend and snide comment about marriage vows. After that he decided he wasn't cut out for "open relationships" and decided to wait until he and Belinda officially ended their marriage.

The sight of Nita brought back a faint feeling of embarrassment. Along with the same fierce tug of attraction. Maybe fiercer.

He stole a look at her behind the wheel. She wore simple white jeans and a cobalt-blue top that set off her tight, graceful body. An air of drive and tension clung to her, but he didn't mind that. An adrenaline junkie himself, he liked women who were passionate about what they did. He'd admired various female paramedics and doctors—from a distance, of course. Despite Belinda's permission, he'd never strayed. Too damn complicated. Not fair to Alison.

But even though he wasn't married now, chances were Nita still thought he was a dick.

Settling into the back seat, he watched her slender hands manipulate the gear shift to back them out of the parking spot. He sincerely hoped he didn't spend his whole time on Santa Lucia staring at her. At least Melissa was ignoring him now, which was a huge improvement over the way she'd stormed at him on the ferryboat.

In the front seat, Nita was telling Melissa about Senator Stryker. "He's mortified. He didn't know where to turn. I mean, who knew he had an inner drag queen just dying to get out?"

"You didn't suspect?"

"No! He's always been so strait-laced and dull. His nickname in Sacramento was Senator Sleeping Pill. Now it's Senator Spanx. It makes you wonder if you ever really know anyone. A lot of things make you wonder that," she added, somewhat bitterly.

Melissa shook her head. "I bet you're mad as hell at the man, after the years you've put in with him."

"At first I just felt bad for him, because he seemed so humbled. He was completely embarrassed. I found him this out-of-the-way, oddball inn where no one will ever think to look for him. The owner, Angie, seems to be a little senile. Either senile or very whimsical. She sings to the flowers in her garden. Also, she thinks Stryker is Clint Eastwood. Or Jeff Bridges, depending on the time of day."

"He must be eating that up. He never had a small ego problem. Has he been driving you crazy?"

"It's definitely made me think. He's like a teenager who got grounded. He keeps making excuses . . ." Nita hesitated, sucked in her cheek, then glanced in the rearview mirror. Her eyes were so beautiful. Bright and dark and swimming with expression. Oops, he was staring. "I'll tell you everything later," she said warily.

"Oh, you mean him?" Melissa tossed a look of annoyance over her shoulder. "If he's anything like Brody—and he probably is, because he's a fire captain too, and Brody raves about him—he'll be stuck to me like toilet paper on my shoe. Brody sent him. Everyone does what Brody says."

"He asked me for a favor," said Jeb, getting annoyed. "Which I interrupted my vacation to do, by the way." Brody owed him, big-time.

"You know, Melissa," Nita said, "I just thought of

something. Angie can really use some help around the Enchanted Garden. She does pretty well considering she's over eighty. I've been doing everything I can, but my fix-it skills are minimal. A man would come in very handy."

Was that a wink? Yes, sexy Nita had winked at him in the rear-view mirror. A completely inappropriate body part responded.

A slow smile spread across his face. He dipped his head in silent thanks. She was trying to help him out, as he'd asked her to.

It worked, too. Melissa changed her tune instantly. "Really, he can be useful as something other than a watchdog? That's different, then. Jeb, do you mind giving Nita a hand?"

He raised his eyebrow at Nita, infusing the gesture with as much teasing intention as he could. "My hands are all hers."

She made a face at him in the rear-view mirror. Even with a scrunched forehead, she appealed to him. He was enjoying their conversation-by-mirror. It was as if an entire silent discussion was taking place out of Melissa's view.

Melissa shifted back and forth on her seat. "How far is it? The bathroom situation is getting dire."

Nita pointed vaguely ahead. "Oh, not far. And the drive is very scenic. It's one of my favorite parts of the island, and—"

Jeb leaned forward. "You don't understand. She needs a bathroom *now*." He'd never forget Belinda's champion peeing. "Anything closer?"

For the first time, Melissa gave him a look that wasn't angry, her green eyes glowing with something suspiciously like gratitude. Nita swung the wheel to the side and pulled into the nearest parking lot, which happened to belong to the Santa Lucia Volunteer Fire Department.

"You've got to be kidding," Melissa groaned. "More firemen? Is anywhere safe?"

"Come on." Jeb jumped out and opened the door for her. He helped her out, then hurried her into the building, which was painted a light pink. Inside, a young, sandy-haired sprout in uniform jumped to his feet.

"Ladies room?" Jeb asked, or rather, *ordered* in the captain's voice of authority that never failed. "I'm Captain Jeb Stone from the San Gabriel Fire Department and this woman needs a bathroom." Melissa seemed to be focused entirely on not peeing, and didn't say a word, not even a protest at how Jeb was taking charge.

The young firefighter, mouth agape, pointed down the hall. Jeb hustled Melissa to the bathroom, shoved her inside, then stood with his back to the door, arms crossed, like some kind of Secret Service officer.

Nita hurried to join him, her eyes wide with alarm. "Is she okay?"

"Far as I know. I'm sure she'll tell us if she isn't."

"You . . . how did you know about the bathroom . . ."

"I have a daughter," he said. "She's nineteen now, but I still remember what those last weeks of pregnancy were like."

A funny expression crossed her face. "Did you do this for your wife? Bundle her into random bathrooms?"

"Once we didn't make it to a bathroom. I found her a nice shrub."

She studied him as if he was some sort of zoo animal. At this close range, he saw that his initial impression had been correct. Not only did she look more tired than she had at the wedding, but more sad as well. It showed in the slump of her shoulders and the way her smile didn't quite engage her whole mouth. He wondered if Mr. Millionaire was to blame.

"Was that . . . I don't know . . . weird? Awkward? Uncomfortable?" she asked.

"I think she was mostly relieved, actually."

"I mean for you."

She was standing about an arm's length from him, but she was leaning in so close that he caught the fresh fragrance of her skin. There was something very clean about her. Clean and bright, like a piece of sea glass tumbled by the ocean. Made him want to dirty her up a little. Like against the wall, right here, right now.

Shove it, Stone, he told himself sternly. He wasn't going to make a fool of himself again.

Her eyes, the deep bronze of strongly brewed tea, were still fixed on him. Right, she was waiting for an answer to her bizarre question. "A woman taking a leak is not weird to me, no. I see all sorts of things in my job. Even at eighteen, I knew girls had bladders too."

"You were a teenage father, then."

"Yeah." Where the hell was she headed with these questions? They seemed very personal. Not that he minded, because she'd taken another mini-step closer to

him and his body was very aware of that fact. Unnerv-
ingly so.

"Were you . . . I mean, was it . . . Never mind."

"Oh no, you don't. You've got me curious now. There's
a reason behind all those questions. You ought to just tell
me what it is."

"Maybe I'm just curious."

"You don't know me, and we're talking about peeing
in the bushes."

She started to laugh, then covered her mouth with one
hand, as if she'd shocked herself. His sense of intrigue
deepened. It looked to him as if she hadn't laughed in a
while.

"You don't know me from Adam, so what's it going to
hurt?" he added.

Her forehead creased in a frown. "Why do you want
to know? Most men would rather skip the whole bare-
your-soul routine."

He could say he wasn't most men, but that wasn't
really true. On the dates he'd been on since the divorce,
he'd listened to his share of sob stories. Apparently that's
what dating was these days. You met someone, ordered
sushi and explained that your father had abandoned you
at the age of thirteen and you'd never gotten over it. After
a certain amount of sake, you explained why that meant
you were into bondage. By the time the green tea sorbet
arrived, your date, if he was Captain Jeb Stone, was about
to self-mutilate.

But for some reason, he sincerely wanted to know what
was motivating Nita's questions and making her sad.

Blame it on the rearview mirror. Or the way she'd looked in that bridesmaid's dress.

She was still watching him steadily. Almost absent-mindedly, she tucked a stray strand of hair behind her ear. She wore no makeup, and a light sheen of sweat dampened her skin, as if she'd been working hard before rushing to the dock to pick them up. His gaze dropped to her mouth, which had an elegantly elongated upper lip. The rest of her screamed busy, on-the-go working woman, but the shape of her mouth said dreamer, with a dash of sensualist.

He wanted to kiss that mouth. Feel its soft give. Tease her passion to the surface.

The sudden bite of lust nearly made him stagger. And the thing was, it wasn't her physical presence that caused it—at least not just that. It was the way she was looking at him, so intently, so curiously. He felt her attention like the stroke of a tongue on his cock.

But Melissa chose that moment to emerge from the bathroom. She was looking much more cheerful. And grateful.

"Come here, Captain Stone."

He turned, taken off guard, as she planted a kiss on his cheek.

"I was wrong. It takes a big woman to admit it, but I clearly qualify." She patted her stomach. "I hate to blame the pregnancy hormones, but my moods have been all over the place. I'm sorry if I was unkind earlier. And thank you, from the bottom of my heart. I already texted Brody and told him he's forgiven. Seriously, I wouldn't have made it without you. Brody thanks you too. And the baby." She beamed at him.

He couldn't see that he'd done much, but he appreciated the change of attitude. Then again, he knew it might not last long. Melissa would probably find something else to be irritated by within the next half hour. The last month of pregnancy had been endless for Belinda. "What are highly-trained, experienced fire captains for, if not to escort pregnant ladies to the restroom?" He offered her his arm. "Shall we?"

"We shall. Nita, I take back every mean thing I said about firefighters. They're the best. Sweet, helpful, manly . . ." She blinked rapidly, then wiped away a tear. Clearly hormone-related. "What am I missing, Jeb?"

Since he preferred antagonistic Melissa to sentimental Melissa, he said, "You left out 'always right'. Not to mention 'irresistible to women.'" He winked at Nita, who creased her forehead with exaggerated skepticism.

"You're not going to make me mad, Jeb. You're still on my good side. Like it or not."

"See?" he muttered to Nita as he and Melissa swept past. "Irresistible."

She made a face at him. Maybe she meant it to be cute, but he found it outrageously sexy. Every cell of his body was aware of her following behind him and Melissa. It was an amazing feeling—revitalizing, as if he was waking up after a long coma in a cave somewhere. He was far more interested in her than in anyone he'd met over the last year. But he couldn't get a read on what she thought about him. Maybe she still saw him as an inappropriate flirt.

Clearly, he was going to have to do something about this situation.

HE DIDN'T GET a chance to formulate a plan until later that night. The Enchanted Garden was a fantastical, cedar-shingled building with a turret and a wraparound front veranda. Gardens surrounded it with a riot of towering blue delphiniums and rampaging rosebushes in every shade of pink, from mauve to coral. Flowering vines twirled around every available pillar or post. The owner must have the greenest thumb ever granted to a human.

Apparently the owner also had an obsession with crafts. When Jeb stepped inside, he was sure he'd stumbled into the mother ship of ruffles. Every spare inch of the place—the bedrooms, the hallways, the bathrooms, even the damn garage—was adorned with frill or lace. Doilies had multiplied like bunnies on every piece of furniture.

When he first saw the dining room, filled with little round tables as if it were a real restaurant, hope flared that he might be able to get a drink. Nita informed him it was called the Knit, Purl, and Tea, and that's what it served, along with the occasional batch of cookies.

Jeb texted Brody a picture of the dainty little room, along with the words, "You owe me, dude." In the midst of all those ruffles, the word "dude" looked like profanity.

Angie was already asleep, but she'd left a rambling note for Nita about all the things that needed to be done the next day.

"Are you working for her?" Melissa asked with a frown, looking as if she was ready for bed too.

Nita shrugged. "You know me. Control freak who likes to keep busy. I've been helping her out. It's better than listening to Stryker rant about the injustice of it all."

With perfect timing, the man in question strolled in, a large tumbler of Scotch in his fist. Jeb figured he must have smuggled it in, and who could blame him. Senator Stryker was a tall, silver-haired, genial man with a voice like a church organ and a hunted look. He resembled an Episcopalian priest rather than someone who liked to pose in strapless bodysuits. But Jeb knew all too well that most people harbored plenty of secrets.

The senator bestowed an embarrassed smile and a handshake on Jeb, and greeted Melissa as if they were old friends.

"Welcome to our cozy little home away from home," he told them blurrily, opening his arms wide, as if the place belonged to him. "We've been having a marvelous time, haven't we, Nita?"

Nita chewed at the inside of her mouth. He wondered why she did that, and if she even knew she was doing it. Just one of the many things he wanted to explore further.

That night, after tossing ten lace-encased pillows off his bed, he considered his options. Number one: Gut it out and try to ignore Nita for the next few days. He crossed that option off the list. Why should he ignore her? He was free. Mr. Millionaire was history. Why should he resist his attraction to her? Number two: get to know her over the next few days, playing it casual and cool, seeing how it went. The problem with that was he wasn't going to be here for long. He might run out of time and never get anywhere. Number three: lay his cards on the table. Tell her exactly what was on his mind, and put the ball in her court.

Sure, she might be offended. But she might also like his honesty. Especially if he did some of that soul-baring you were supposed to do on dates. Except he'd do it Jeb Stone-style.

Plan formulated, he fell asleep to the soothing scent of rose-petal potpourri.

Chapter Four

UNFORTUNATELY FOR HIS plan, Nita was a hard woman to catch up with. Even holed up on a remote island, she managed to keep herself busy. When she wasn't closeted with the senator, she was assisting Angie in the tearoom or setting up her computer reservations system or locating her knitting needles. While he liked to keep busy too, Jeb caught a whiff of the manic in her compulsion to keep moving.

When Melissa and Senator Stryker disappeared to work on a background interview, Jeb saw his chance. He cornered Angie and Nita in the kitchen. Angie, who wore her snow-white hair piled as high as Marie Antoinette's, was knitting away on a scarf, most of which was already draped around her neck.

"Put me to work," he told them. "I noticed the kitchen sink is leaking. I can fix that."

"Oh, I couldn't possibly allow that," Angie scolded.

"She thinks you're Gregory Peck," explained Nita in a whisper.

"Who does she think you are?"

"Audrey Hepburn." Nita snorted, but Jeb could actually see the resemblance.

"Well, Audrey, I could use some help with the sink. Would you like to play fake plumber's assistant?"

"I suppose it's better than playing fake dead movie star." She smiled at him, and he got the sense that she'd softened toward him. Maybe his bathroom-locating abilities had impressed her.

After they'd convinced Angie that Gregory Peck had no problem with household chores, he found the water shutoff, settled under the sink, and got to work.

"What's my role here?" Nita asked. She crouched next to him, peering under the sink.

"If I say it's to keep me company, will you leave?"

"I have a million things to do . . ."

"I need someone to hand me the tools," he said quickly.

"I have a degree from Bryn Mawr."

"Then you should have no problem with it."

She heaved a sigh and shifted to her knees. Jeb studiously kept his eyes on the pipes above his head. Nita on her knees. Not a helpful image right now.

"Pass the wrench."

It took her a minute to locate the wrench—maybe she'd skipped shop at Bryn Mawr—but in the end she handed him the correct tool.

"That sounded pretentious, didn't it?" she said. "Mentioning Bryn Mawr. Bradford used to do that. He was a master of the degree-drop and the name-drop."

Ah-ha. An opening. "What happened with him? You two looked very ..." He searched for the right word. "Like a real power couple."

Actually, the guy had looked like a weenie to him, but a wealthy one.

"And you looked like a homecoming couple."

"Shows what you know, Bryn Mawr. We weren't ever a homecoming couple. We both got our GEDs. Never went to prom."

She seemed to take that as a challenge. "And we weren't a power couple, fireman. That would require us being an actual couple."

"You were snuggled up pretty close."

"So were you. I saw you on the dance floor. It might as well have been a prom. You probably made out in the parking lot afterward."

He made the sound of a buzzer. "You lose. There was no making out."

"Really? Maybe she was mad because you were flirting with the bridesmaids."

He gritted his teeth. "I wasn't flirting. And I only talked to one bridesmaid." Had there been other bridesmaids? Honestly, he couldn't remember.

"It was three years ago. You can't possibly remember if you talked to other bridesmaids. Or if you made out or not."

"I'm pretty damn sure."

"Why?"

"Are you always like this with the questions?" He twisted a pipe, which came out in his hand.

"No. But I had this idea that you were the perfect couple, the perfect family, and now you tell me you're divorced, and all my illusions are shattered. I'm wondering what happened between then and now. You looked so lovey-dovey together."

Lovey-dovey? He wanted to gag, especially given the true state of things between him and Belinda. "That's funny, because by the time of Brody's wedding we hadn't had sex in two years."

"Two *years*?"

Oh God, now he'd done it. He always did have a knack for brutal honesty, which had its good points and its bad points. Might as well go for broke.

"Or for two years after the wedding. In fact . . ." Why hold anything back? "I haven't had sex for five years."

NITA STARED AT the mouth-watering length of man stretched under the sink. Jeb Stone had been at the Enchanted Garden for the sum total of one night, and already he'd turned all her ideas about him upside down. The man exuded sex from every cell, but he hadn't had sex in five years?

"Why not?"

"Long story, but the gist of it is that my wife— ex-wife—Belinda decided we shouldn't, since we both knew we wouldn't last past Alison's eighteenth birthday."

Nita wondered if she'd been wrong about everything

at Melissa's wedding. She'd certainly been wrong about Bradford.

Jeb continued. "I feel I should warn you that when a man hasn't had sex in five years and he meets a woman he's attracted to, that could be trouble."

A thrill shivered through her. "Trouble how?"

"I'll probably be pulling out all the stops to get you into bed. In fact, I know I will."

"Excuse me?"

"Yep. Brace yourself. Plumber's tape, please."

Slightly stunned, she passed him the only thing that could possibly be plumber's tape. "You're a player, aren't you? You were flirting at the wedding. And now you're doing it again."

"A player?" He let out a bark of a laugh. "That's a good one. And I didn't flirt. I was about to flirt. Never quite got there. It's quite likely I'm flirting now, but since it's been a long time, I'm not sure I'm doing it right."

"Oh, you're doing pretty well," said Nita faintly. Not that she would necessarily call it flirting, but he'd certainly gotten her attention with his direct approach. And held it.

She feasted her eyes on the body stretched out before her. With his arms stretched overhead, his T-shirt rode up, revealing rippling stomach muscles. He inhabited his body in a confident way that made him very easy to look at and talk to. He seemed completely comfortable with himself, and his frankness was addictive. She didn't encounter much frankness in her world.

"So what am I supposed to do with this information?" She asked his prone body.

"Oh no, I'm not telling you what to do. I know better. But if you aren't interested, you might want to tone down *that*."

He gestured at her with his pipe wrench.

"That? What's that?"

"That sexiness. You make it hard on a man."

"You mean, hard on a man who hasn't had sex in five years."

"See, that's the trouble. Is it the five years, or would I have the hots for you no matter what? I figure there's only one way to know."

"What?"

"You should go to bed with me."

Another disturbing thrill raced through her nervous system. "Well, that's convenient. Is that the answer to all life's little mysteries?"

He laughed and settled the new length of black plastic pipe into place. "There's a good chance that's true. At least, it might be the answer to not letting them bother you."

A philosopher/plumber/fireman. Definitely not the type of guy she'd spent time with before.

"Does this line about the five years work with most women?"

"Lines are not my style," he said with a grunt as he secured the pipe. "I'd rather just tell it like it is and take my lumps. And I haven't tried to get any other woman into bed."

Nita's fascination grew. Under discreet questioning, Melissa had said he'd been divorced for a year. He could have crammed a lot of sexual activity into that time. Especially given how scorchingly hot he was. "Why haven't you slept with anyone?"

"If I wanted to have sex just to have sex, I would have by now. I'm not looking for that."

"Uh-huh." In her experience, men were looking almost exclusively for that.

"I'm serious. When you feel that zing, that's when things get interesting. And when I look at you, I feel the zing."

If the "zing" was this giddy feeling ping-ponging around her body, she definitely felt it too. "What about your ex-wife? No zing?"

"We had a different kind of zing. The kind that makes your head explode when you're seventeen. This isn't that kind." He dabbed some kind of goop on the pipe and climbed out from under the sink. The pipe had dripped water on his T-shirt, which clung to his muscles. He had outstanding muscles. She wanted to tear that shirt off and touch each and every one of them.

"What's our kind of zing?" There was no point in pretending there wasn't a zing. They both felt it, and neither was bothering to hide it. Especially not Jeb.

"The kind where I want to find out what your favorite flavor of ice cream is, and whether you like Shane Black movies and who your first crush was and why you looked so sad when you asked me about Melissa and the bathroom."

She stared at him, totally thrown for a loop. Had she really looked sad? Of course she *was* sad, but she didn't like to dump that on anyone else. "I think I've realized something. You're not a normal man."

"Are you insulting me or complimenting me?"

"Just . . . uh . . . getting to know you."

"Well, good. Getting to know each other is important, especially if we intend to go to bed together." He winked at her. Heat shivered between her thighs.

"I'm not going to jump into bed with you because you haven't had sex in five years."

"You'd better not. That would be a terrible reason. I promise I'll come up with much better reasons than that. Look, I'm stuck here until Melissa's done with her interview. I thought we could look at the next few days as one long date."

"I never sleep with a man on the first date."

He leaned in, bracing one hand on the wall behind her. His dark hair was cropped short, maybe two degrees away from a buzz cut. He had the look of someone who'd seen a lot in his time, and who didn't put up with crap. A smudge of dust on his cheekbone somehow set off his eyes, making them look even more tigerish than before. "Maybe that's because you've never had a date with me."

She felt the breath whoosh out of her. No, she hadn't. Or with anyone remotely like him.

He gave a little smile, clearly satisfied with the effect he'd had. "So, what's next on Angie's honey-do list?"

Nita consulted the scrap of paper she'd shoved in her pocket. "Garden gate's off its hinges. The place has a gardener, but he refuses to deal with anything that's not plant-related."

Jeb crossed to the shut-off valve and turned the water back on. "Does Angie have more carpentry tools?"

"She has a tool shed. I rummaged around and found some stuff. They're already out there. I like to be organized."

"See, I knew we were perfect for each other. I like an organized firehouse."

She mimed checking something off a list. "Likes organization, check."

"I get points for fixing the pipe, don't I?"

She felt a smile tremble at the corners of her mouth. "Skilled with his hands, check."

His eyes heated to a molten gold. "Now you're just teasing me."

"You backing out of the date?"

"Hell no. And I think we just made it past the appetizers."

She laughed, and it felt so good, like a bright bubble bursting in her chest. During the last year, between job stress and personal stress, she hadn't done much laughing.

She led the way through the Knit, Purl, and Tea, wincing at the reek of the rose-petal essential oil Angie liked to sprinkle on the tablecloths. The Enchanted Garden had never looked so feminine as it did now, with rough and rugged Jeb Stone striding around in it.

But for once, another man sat in the Knit, Purl, and Tea. He was young, sandy-haired, and looked vaguely familiar. His knees barely fit under the dainty little round table. At the sight of Jeb, he leaped to his feet and dashed across the room. The table nearly went flying.

"Captain Stone," the kid said.

Jeb did a double take. "You know me?"

"I saw you at the station. When you came in to use the bathroom."

"Right. How are you?"

"I'm Charlie Scott. I'm a volunteer firefighter and me and the other guys want to know—"

"No," said Jeb.

"But you don't even—"

"Whatever it is, no. I'm on vacation. And on baby-watch. And on a date." He slanted a teasing look at Nita, who grinned. Lord, she liked this man.

But the kid persisted. "All we want to know is if you'll give us some extra training. See, the fire chief . . ." he lowered his voice, "he drinks a lot. He doesn't teach us anything. We've been renting action movies so we can see how real firefighters do it, but we still have a few questions."

Jeb looked pained. He shot Nita a silent plea for help. She shrugged, wanting to do some teasing of her own. "It's true about the fire chief, I know that much. The knitting circle's always complaining about it."

"A lot of people are hoping he falls off the wharf on his way home from Old Mort's," said Charlie cheerfully. "Wouldn't be surprised to see someone give him a push. Unless they get some real training, that is."

Nita snorted. The indelicate sound seemed to make the lace curtains shudder. "Are you telling Jeb the chief's life is in his hands?"

Charlie looked hopeful. "Will that work?"

"No," said Jeb. "Anyway, I don't have time to train anyone. I'm only here for a few days."

"But even a little bit would help, especially from one of the Bachelor Firemen. My girlfriend has a whole scrapbook on you guys . . . oops, I wasn't supposed to tell you."

Nita swung toward Jeb. "A Bachelor Fireman. How could I forget?" She leaned in to whisper in his ear. "Do I get a prize for going on a date with a Bachelor Fireman?"

"Yes." He quirked one eyebrow. "You can claim your prize tonight."

She flushed. If he was rusty at flirting, she'd hate to see him in top form. "Sorry, Charlie," she told the young fireman. "This fire captain is already spoken for. Maybe you can have him later." Circling his wrist, she tugged him across the room. The feel of his warm flesh and the solid bones underneath made her oddly happy.

A wind chime jangled as they walked out the front door, into the charming front yard, which was enclosed by a white gingerbread fence. Roses tumbled over little stone benches, while a sculpted Cupid poured water into a mossy fountain. Lanterns hung in the lemon trees. Truth to tell, she'd booked the place solely because of this garden with its white cabbage roses and velvet-hearted black-eyed Susans.

She inhaled the fragrance, letting it seep into her being. Maybe when she got back to work she'd make a habit of keeping flowers at her desk.

Right. As if she'd ever have time for that.

By the sidewalk, the gate stood off its hinges, one end resting on the grass. Jeb knelt down next to it and peered at the hinges. "The wood's rotten. The hinge came right through it."

"Great. What do we do?"

He gave it a long, thorough scrutiny that made her wonder what it would feel like if he looked at her like that. While she was naked.

"I could build one."

"You can *build* a gate?"

"Sure. It's not complicated. Pretty simple design. But it'll take some time. I can also just replace this one piece here." He tapped the offending post. "If Angie has any extra lumber lying around, I can take a look."

Nita beckoned him toward a path that wound around the side of the building. "Let's check the tool shed."

As she led the way, she could swear he was checking out her ass. Fair enough, since she'd scoped him out a few times. She added some sway to her stride. Talk about rusty. When was the last time she'd tried to look sexy for a man? Probably early-Bradford era.

It seemed to be working on Jeb, because when she glanced back, she caught him watching her with a little frown between his eyebrows. But his next question wasn't flirtatious. "Do you like working for Senator Stryker?"

An easy question, easy answer. She opened her mouth, but nothing came out. Where was her automatic "yes, of course"? Her "it's a dream come true"? Or "it's an incredible opportunity"?

"I was the first Hispanic press secretary Senator Stryker ever hired. He's California's longest-serving State Senator and very influential."

"That's impressive."

"I've always wanted to shine, to prove myself."

"I'm sure you've done it."

She hadn't answered the question. He probably realized it, but didn't push. Nibbling at the inside of her cheek, she wondered why she hadn't given her usual answer. Was it because it had stopped being true? Was it because she couldn't lie to someone as forthright as Jeb Stone?

Reaching the shed, she undid the latch and opened the door. Jeb stepped inside, gave a quick scan, then turned to face her. The only light came from the open door, which made the little building soothingly dim, a welcome break from the vivid sunshine outside. There was barely room for the two of them, and suddenly even the dust motes seemed to quiver from the energy vibrating between them. She took an involuntary step back and hit the door jamb.

He cocked his head, as if trying to make out what she was feeling. Then he slowly offered his hand to her, palm up. An offering? An invitation? Whatever it was, she hesitated only a moment before placing her hand carefully in his. Slowly, surely, he tugged her toward him until nothing separated their bodies except their clothes and a humming layer of air. He kept his hand clasped with hers.

"I want to kiss you," he murmured. "But I see you might be wary."

She was staring at his chest—his husky, broad chest—hugged by the still-damp, hunter green T-shirt. Lifting her gaze, she passed the neckline of his shirt, a scattering of dark hair peeking out, the strong tendons of his neck, his firm jaw, and fastened on the mouth that had fascinated her from the beginning.

"Should I be? Wary?"

"That all depends on what scares you." With his free hand, he brushed her hair away from her face. "You know what I want. What do you want?"

That was the thing. She couldn't have what she wanted. All her passionate love, all her hard work, all her carefulness, hadn't kept disaster at bay. For a moment, the harsh grief threatened, like a demon clutching at her soul. But then there was this man standing before her, a man like no one she'd ever met, and he was looking at her steadily, unafraid, attentive. Wanting her.

Rising onto her tiptoes, steadying herself with a hand on his shoulder, she lifted her face to his. Carefully, gently, she pressed her mouth against those beautifully formed lips of his. He tasted like . . . life. Like fresh orange juice and a morning breeze off the ocean. A soft, melting effect stole across her senses. He didn't open his mouth, but simply moved his head from side to side, a tiny shift that brought delicious sensation in its wake.

She sighed as her body relaxed against his. He was holding her now with both hands, a solid clasp that promised not to let her down. Her torso met his, the intimate contact of her breasts against his chest making her tremble. Those strong hands made circles on her back—slow, arousing circles.

He smelled so good, a whiff of coffee mixed with spicy aftershave. She wanted to bury her head in his neck, nuzzle against the warm flesh there. But she also didn't want to budge from where she was, that magical space in which her mouth pressed against his. It was a little bit sulky, that lower lip, a little James Dean, a little Jim Morrison. He had the mouth of a rock god, of a man who'd drawn women to him since puberty, of a man completely confident in his own manhood.

She opened her lips, swiped her tongue against his lower lip. He gave a little growl, which scraped across her nerve endings. Then he gently caught her lower lip in his teeth, and those nerve endings pulsed into triple overdrive. Her heart raced with an unfamiliar emotion.

Desire.

She'd forgotten what it felt like. It felt astonishing, like a favorite song she hadn't heard in years. Or a favorite color. *Red. How could I have forgotten that I love the color red? How did I live without red?* He explored her mouth with commanding assurance, as if he knew exactly how much turmoil his tongue and lips were generating. As if he wanted every part of her to vibrate with excitement, tremble with anticipation.

As she tilted her head back, abandoning herself to his kiss—was it a kiss, or a statement of purpose?—her thoughts took on a cartwheeling, giddy quality. *How could I have forgotten there's something in this world that feels so good? I'm alive, I'm alive. So good. But has it ever felt this good before? Did I forget that I'm a woman, not a medical project?*

That thought acted more or less like a shower of ice cubes on the moment. She tore her mouth away from his, knowing it was wet and swollen, knowing how turned-on she looked. Putting a trembling hand to her lips, she felt tears spring to her eyes. Quickly, she blinked them away. *Don't notice, don't notice*, she pleaded silently.

Fat chance. Jeb Stone didn't miss a trick. His eyes narrowed in concern. "Was I out of line?"

She shook her head, still beyond words. Struggling for a grip on her unruly emotions, she trailed a hand on his chest, lingering over the spot where his heart beat fast and steady. He covered her hand with his.

"What is it?" He asked gently, as if he really wanted to know. And that was what undid her. Even knowing that their "date" might end after one great kiss, she couldn't resist the worry in his gold-striped eyes.

But she had to look away before she could say it. Fixing her gaze on a row of hammers on a pegboard, she braced herself and said, "Bradford left me because I got pregnant. He wasn't interested in having a child with me. Then, when I was four months along, I lost the baby."

Chapter Five

NITA HAD HER eyes squeezed shut, as if afraid to face him after her revelation. Jeb cupped her face in one hand and brushed his thumb against her mouth, still plump from his kiss.

"That's rough," he said. "Really rough. Are you doing okay now?"

"Better," she said cautiously, opening one eye a sliver and looking almost surprised to see him.

"I'm still here," he reassured her. "Did you think I wouldn't be?"

She opened both eyes. "It's not exactly first-date entertainment material."

"I asked, remember? I asked because I wanted to know." Now that he knew, he wasn't entirely sure what to do. Clearly she was still raw from the whole experience. "I knew Bradford was an ass."

Maybe he'd picked the right tack, because she managed a smile. "He wasn't a total ass. Maybe about seventy-percent ass. He said he'd pay child support. I decided to have the baby by myself, even though my mother cried for a week. But I'm smart and capable, right? I was scared, but happy too. Then, at about sixteen weeks along, it all just ended. There was an infection, and I had to go to the hospital. The doctor said it happens."

She looked so slim and wounded standing there in the shadowy shed where he'd kissed the hell out of her. Had she really gone through all that alone? "And Bradford? What happened to him?"

"He sent me a condolence email." A wry smile tugged at one corner of her mouth. "He couldn't disappear fast enough when I got pregnant. That's why I was so fascinated by how you helped Melissa. I don't think Bradford's ever a found a woman a bush to pee on."

"To be accurate, she peed behind the bush, not on it."

The smile gathered steam, dragging the other corner of her mouth along with it. Her eyes sparkled from a light sheen of tears. "Thanks for the clarification."

"And if that had been me, you wouldn't have been able to tear me away." The words came out much more fiercely than he'd intended. But it was true. When Belinda had gotten pregnant, he'd married her and they'd centered their lives around Alison. Even now, knowing the truth about Belinda, he didn't regret it. He couldn't imagine making any other choice. "Not to judge the guy. Everyone has his road. But I wouldn't have picked that one."

"Well. I don't blame him. My mother said it was my

fault for waiting so long and caring about my career too much."

"Ouch."

"Yeah. Well. Moments like this, when the man I work for has become a laughing-stock, it's hard to argue."

She gave herself a brisk shake, as if throwing off her blue mood. He wondered if their kiss had made her sad. He didn't want that to happen. Maybe he should try another one, see if he could get a different result. Something more in the line of blissful. That seemed a little risky, though. The moment for kissing had passed. He should return to his handyman approach.

He cast his eyes around the shed and located a post that he could easily cut down to the proper size for the gate. Picking it up, he hefted it in his hand, testing for rot. "One gate repair, coming up. And by the way, I think we've successfully made it through dinner."

Her face lit with a smile so dazzling, it made him lightheaded. "Really? Good. Because I'm already eyeing dessert." She raised an eyebrow and looked him up and down, quick as a wink.

And just like that, he was hard again, hard and aching, just as he'd been during the kiss that had just about knocked him on his ass. "Zing" didn't nearly cover it.

AFTER SPENDING MUCH of the morning directing Jeb through Angie's list of household repairs, Nita bumped into Melissa in the breakfast room, where she was going over notes on her laptop. She had to sit sideways because her belly didn't fit under the tiny round tables.

This time, the pang of envy wasn't nearly what it had been. Jeb's easy acceptance of her story made a difference. He'd treated her with the same degree of teasing interest after her revelation as before. He still saw her as a desirable woman, instead of as a pitiable failure.

So maybe she had been a little harsh on herself.

Nita drew up a chair and helped herself to one of the powdered-sugar almond cookies Melissa was devouring.

"How's the interview coming?" She asked her friend.

"We're about to go on camera. He's doing his makeup now." Melissa quirked a smile at her. "That phrase takes on a whole new meaning, knowing what we now know. You won't mind if I make him sweat, will you?"

"Don't hold back on my account. This is between him and the public. And the online drag queen community. And the makers of Spanx. Allegedly."

"Yeah, well, I was just going through the photos, and I think we're way past allegedly. We're in the 'OMG, no he didn't' range. He gives Lady Gaga a run for her money."

Nita winced. "If only he hadn't posted those stupid selfies online. The Internet is a dangerous thing when you think you're one step down from God Almighty."

"Nita! I'm shocked. I've never heard you talk about the senator that way."

"Yeah, well, I've never been stranded on an island with him before. It's given me a whole new take on his character."

Melissa leaned in, then winced a little as her belly

squished against the table. "I really appreciate the tip. I haven't been able to work as much as I want, and it's been driving me crazy. Brody calls me every two minutes when he's on shift. At home he acts like some fire-breathing dragon guarding the cave."

"But things are good?" Nita asked, a little worried.

"Oh yes," Melissa answered quickly. "I'm not really complaining. I love that man. I know he's just being extra-protective. I mean, sending Jeb Stone out here? Come on. Who does that?"

Nita felt a distinct sense of warmth in her cheeks. "He doesn't seem so bad."

"Oh." After a quick glance, Melissa sat back. "You like him."

The warmth increased. "I barely know him."

"He makes an impact."

"That he does." Nita nibbled on a cookie, watching the powdered sugar float onto the tablecloth. She decided to put her cards on the table, the way Jeb would. "What do you know about him?"

"I know Brody likes him, and that's enough for me. I know he's putting his daughter through an expensive college and that he let his wife take most of their possessions in the divorce."

"What's she like?" Nita tried to sound casual, but failed completely. What kind of woman would walk away from a man like Jeb Stone? She was having a hard time wrapping her mind around it.

"Belinda?" Melissa gave a quick glance around the empty tea room. "She's . . . pretty. Really into tennis.

Kind of bubbly. Has a lot in common with . . . um, Ellen DeGeneres."

It took a moment for Nita to make the connection. "What are you saying, that she's . . . *really*?"

"Just my own personal, private speculation that I'm sharing only with you. As a little thank you for the tip. Not to be shared with anyone." Melissa made a zipping motion across her lips. "I've never even wondered aloud in Brody's presence. I figure it's not our business. And since Jeb never said a word, it's especially not our business."

"Do you think he knows?"

"Not much gets past Jeb."

"That's . . . uh, wow." Boy, had she been off the mark. She did a slow burn, thinking of her snap judgments about Jeb and his wife. "I feel like a fool. At the wedding, I thought they were a perfect-looking couple."

Melissa grinned. "I knew he caught your eye."

"I wonder why they stayed together so long."

"Well, I also happen to know that both Jeb and Belinda's parents were missionaries, and that he's not the kind of man who would walk away from a marriage, especially if that would mean exposing any secrets his wife might be keeping from her family."

"Wow," said Nita, again. "You are quite the investigative reporter, aren't you?"

Melissa laughed. "That's a compliment, right?"

"Of course. Just remind me not to be too revealing around you."

From Melissa's suddenly self-conscious look, she realized it was too late. "Oh hell. You know about my miscarriage?"

"Only if you want me to." Melissa spoke from behind the tea cup she'd quickly raised to her lips.

Nita struggled for a moment, chewing on her cheek. Melissa was her friend. But could an eight months' pregnant woman truly understand? On the other hand, she'd told Jeb—at least the basic facts—so why shouldn't she also tell her dear friend? "I should have told you. I'm not sure how much you know, but it was horrible. I ended up in the hospital and lost a lot of blood. It was scary."

Melissa went pale, her green eyes dark with worry. "My God, Nita. Are you okay?"

Nita fixed her gaze on the table, worried that too much sympathy would make her lose it. She did much better when she was moving, moving, moving. "I'm fine now. I couldn't tell anyone, I . . . I felt like such a failure. Bradford dumped me as soon as I got pregnant. I was so wrong about him, I couldn't believe I'd been so stupid. I just . . . lost so much confidence in myself. I barely felt like a woman anymore."

"Oh, Nita." Melissa put a warm hand over hers. "I'm so, so sorry. Oh, crap. Here I go." She mopped at her eyes. "This is partly for you, partly because I keep bursting into tears at random moments. You know that I never thought Bradford was worthy. Did you love him?"

Nita thought about it, really thought about it. "I think I did, in a way, but I also never felt at home with him. If that makes sense. Do you know I never let him see me without makeup? Even when he spent the night?"

DESPERATELY SEEKING FIREMAN 57

"Hmm," said Melissa wisely. "The no-makeup test. An essential part of the courtship process."

Amazingly, Nita chuckled, feeling another microscopic lightening of her heart. "I'm really glad you're here, Melissa. Maybe I ought to thank the senator."

"Of course you should thank me. But thank me for what?" Senator Stryker loomed over them, barely recognizable under layers of foundation. He wasn't scowling at her, perhaps because he was afraid to disturb his makeup.

Nita jumped to her feet. "I was just telling Melissa I ought to thank you for talking to her. I wasn't sure if I had already."

"Hm." Vanity gratified, the senator gestured to Melissa. "I'm as ready as I'm going to be. Nita, you have my talking points?"

"They're on my computer."

"Well, I just got off the phone with my lawyer, and he advises against going on camera at all."

Melissa looked a little alarmed by that, though Nita shot her a reassuring glance. She knew from experience that once the senator had donned the makeup, there was no going back. "You'll do fine," she told him. "If lawyers had their way, no one would ever talk. And then how would you get publicity? Get the audience on your side. Be charming. Apologetic. A little humble. You can do this, Senator."

He gave a brusque nod. It didn't matter what the lawyer said, he knew as well as she did that he needed to make some sort of public statement. They couldn't stay at the Enchanted Garden forever.

Although the thought of leaving this place made her unexpectedly sad.

"Where do we set up, Melissa?"

"My camera's out by that little bench in the front. It's shaded and quiet. It'll show people another side of you."

"Showing another side of me is what got me into this mess." He winked, and a puff of powder drifted into the air.

Melissa and Nita burst into surprised laughter. "If you say that on camera, I'm quitting," Nita said.

From the senator's jovial smile, the one he reserved for upper-level staff members, she knew he didn't believe her. But for the rest of the afternoon, the words "I'm quitting" ricocheted around her brain. Was she, shocker of shockers, considering quitting? Why? What would she do? Her job was all she had anymore. Why would she want to quit?

JEB TOOK A break from his handyman duties to help Angie in the Knit, Purl and Tea. This became necessary when Angie plopped down at a table with five of her friends, apparently forgetting she had anything to do with running the place. He brought the ladies a pot of tea, which delighted them so much that he made a joke of it and donned a frilly apron. That's when things got ugly. They set about trying to determine his marital status and suitability for their single female relatives. An hour later his apron pockets were stuffed with phone numbers scrawled on scraps of napkin.

Finally—hallelujah—Nita walked into the room, looking lip-smackingly good in a light blue sundress that bared her long, tan legs. She stopped in her tracks, gave him a lingering, incredulous once-over, then burst into laughter.

He wanted to be offended, but the joy in her face made him so happy, he couldn't. Her dark hair flowed down her back, just begging to be released from that ponytail. Why did women like ponytails? He'd never understand that. One strand had come out of her hair tie and bounced against her shoulder as she rocked with laughter.

Okay, enough was enough. He strode toward her, in as manly a manner as he could with that darn apron around his hips. "You're disturbing my customers," he told her with a scowl. "Now if you'd like to place an order, that's different."

"If you say 'coffee, tea, or me' I'm going to totally lose it."

"Sadly, the Knit, Purl, and Tea doesn't serve anything as stimulating as coffee. We draw the line at black tea. How about some Earl Grey with an estrogen chaser?"

The corners of her eyes were wet from laughing; she swiped at first one, then the other, letting out a sigh. "It's nice for the ladies to have a place where they can be themselves."

Jeb glanced over at his table of six, three of whom were checking out his ass. He reached into the apron pocket and brandished a handful of scribbled numbers at her. "Being themselves apparently means hitting on me."

She took the scraps of paper from him, frowning.

"That seems inappropriate. I don't like to see the staff treated like this."

"I'm not the staff," he growled, then stopped short. The word "staff" echoed between them, hovering between joke and suggestive double entendre. She picked up on it too, judging by the pink that appeared in her cheeks. Once, twice, she opened her mouth, then closed it again. Finally she cleared her throat.

"Well, I have a manlier task for you, if you're interested."

"Hmm, let me ask my balls." He paused. "The answer's yes."

She gave a delighted little chuckle that seemed to reach right to his cock. "There's an order of supplies coming in on the next ferry. Can you drive down with me and help load it up?"

"Can I do it wearing a frilly apron?"

"No."

"Then I'm in. Let me just check on Melissa first."

"She's fine. She's with the senator, asking him follow-up questions."

"Thanks, but she's still my main responsibility here. I'll do a quick visual check, then meet you at the van."

He wasn't sure why that made her laugh, but once again, he didn't mind at all.

Chapter Six

THE WORD ON the wharf was that the ferryboat was going to be nearly an hour late.

"Some big swells out there," one of the old fishermen told them. "Could be a storm coming."

"It's only September," said Nita with a frown. "Don't the storms start up in December?"

But the man had already moved on. Jeb took Nita by the elbow as they made their way back up the ramp to the wharf parking lot. "I can think of something to do with that hour."

"Really?" One slim dark eyebrow rose meaningfully. "Are you thinking of pulling a shift at the nail salon?"

"I swear I'm never putting on a damn apron again. I was thinking we could take a quick tour of the island."

"A tour? That sounds so . . . touristy."

"I am on vacation, after all. When's the last time you had a vacation?"

With her hand on the door handle of the Suburban, she cocked her head, considering the question. "Where have I heard that before? Oh right. My mother."

He let out a curse. "Fucking apron. Never again."

She laughed, throwing her head back. If you asked him, she was getting better at the laughing thing. Maybe it was like riding a bicycle. Or like sex. A pleasant little flare of anticipation flickered in his belly.

"Hop in," she said. "Let's take a tour."

As he slid into the passenger seat, he remembered his rented Maserati, now sitting in a parking garage on the mainland. He thought about the girls who had checked him out, the interested glances he'd collected up and down the Pacific Coast Highway. And he realized he'd rather be right where he was. In a rattletrap Suburban driven by the sexy, incredibly appealing Nita Moreno.

The "zing." It was all about the "zing."

Nita steered the van along the road that ran through town. She gave him a rapid run-through of the highlights—the town hall, the best fish burger in town, the Maritime Museum, the original homestead from the island's first settlers. As they passed the fire station, she said, "By the way, the fire chief stopped me at the grocery store. He said you're to keep the hell away from his crew."

He shook his head as they rumbled off the pavement onto the gravel road at the edge of town. "Aw, he shouldn't have done that. Now I'm going to have to go."

"Excuse me?" She glanced over at him. The wind from the open window whipped her hair against her cheek, with a few strands getting caught in her mouth. She tried to flick them away with her tongue, a maddeningly sexy effort that did nothing to the hair and everything to his dick.

"Here, let me," he said in a suddenly gruff voice. He reached over and gently tugged the wet hair away from her face. "Where's your hair tie?"

"Don't tell me you do hair too?"

"I wouldn't go that far, but I have opposable thumbs and I know what to do with them."

Her eyelids flickered. Pink appeared on her cheeks. Oh, he was getting to her, he just knew it. She caught her bottom lip between her teeth, giving him another glimpse of her tongue. He remembered the taste of her, sweeter than peaches.

"Don't stop there," she told him, carefully keeping her eyes on the road. "What else do you know how to do with your thumbs?"

"See, I'm not good with words the way you are. I'm better at demonstrating." He took a chance and put his hand on the back of her neck, under the wind-tangled mass of hair. He made a slow circle with his thumb, rubbing the tight tendon he found there.

She made a sound somewhere between a sigh and a groan. "You have no idea how good that feels."

"You don't relax much, do you?"

"Sometimes I do. I watched a Bones marathon just last week while sampling all the Ben & Jerry's flavors the island carries."

"Bones? Isn't that about a coroner? Doesn't sound very relaxing." He ran his thumb down the slope of her neck to her collarbone, found some more tense muscles along the ridge of her shoulder and got to work on those. Her skin felt incredibly soft to him. He'd given Belinda plenty of backrubs over the years, but they'd lost their erotic charge, and her skin didn't have this effect on him. This galvanizing, seductive effect.

"Are you trying to make me pull over?" She tilted her head to the side, offering him more access.

"Is it working?"

"Well, I was going to take you to the abandoned lighthouse. It's at the top of this hill and has an incredible view. I haven't been inside yet."

"Drive," he ordered her, removing his hand from her neck. "I work much better at a stationary location."

They drove in loaded silence. Jeb wanted to burst into song—some sort of triumphant, male victory chant. At the moment, all he wanted in life was to get this woman naked. Images skittered through his brain. Lovely amber skin, long legs, that shadow between her breasts, dark hair falling across her bare breasts, eyes half-lidded in sleepy arousal, her hands reaching into his pants . . .

He made an involuntary sound in the back of his throat.

She whipped her head toward him. "What is it?"

"Just drive fast, would you?"

Closing her mouth with a quick snap, she drove. He stared out the window, determined to get a firmer grip on his excitement. They wound their way up a hill covered in scrubby, low-growing grasses. A few cows grazed among the clumps of grass. Beyond the hill, the periwinkle ocean basked in the sunshine. The setting was pure beauty, and he didn't give a crap. All he wanted was to get to the damn lighthouse.

And then, there they were, pulling up outside a charming little lighthouse, its white paint peeling, its windows cracked. A fence ran along the perimeter, with a big sign that said "Keep Out."

It didn't seem to worry Nita, so Jeb shrugged and followed her around the building. And there, at the side, was a gap in the chain link fence.

"Angie told me about this," said Nita as she ducked through the hole. "It's sort of a Lover's Lane kind of thing. They say if you drive up here and see a car, it's common courtesy to turn right back around. And . . ." She pushed open a door built into the lighthouse. Inside, a cozy little room glowed with hazy sunlight that filtered from slits of windows high above. Cushioned benches ran along each of the six walls. Colorful pillows were piled in one corner, and a stack of blankets filled another. When both of them had stepped inside, she closed the door behind them and turned the lock. "The best part is, it locks from the inside only."

She turned in a slow circle, checking the place out while he checked her out. When she was done, she dragged her gaze to meet his. She caught her bottom lip between her teeth, looking suddenly uncertain. "What are you thinking? Is this stupid? Too much? Bad idea? Too forward?"

Hot lust flooded Jeb's entire being. He wanted to rip her clothes off, spread her open on one of those window seats and fuck her until his head exploded. In two strides, he was beside her. "Not a bad idea," he managed through his lust-tightened throat. "Great idea. Do you mind?"

Somehow, his hands were at the zipper on the back of her sundress, and she was pressed against him, leaning forward so he could unzip her. Underneath he found nothing but smooth skin.

"No bra," he said in a raspy voice, as if he'd smoked a pack of cigarettes in the last second.

"I'm not the bustiest of women," she said, a little shaky.

He worked her dress off her body, watching each inch of skin appear. Sleek thighs, white cotton boy-shorts underwear, a belly with the cutest hint of extra flesh. He paused, soaking her in.

"Could you get me out of here?" Her voice was smothered in sundress.

"Working on it," he murmured, touching the tender skin of her stomach. A shiver rippled across her muscles. She squirmed. "Okay, okay." He lifted the dress the rest of the way, exposing her breasts, perfect little pears just begging to be nibbled. His mouth watered, but he held off until he'd freed her from her clothes.

When she stood mostly naked before him, breathless and tousled, all lovely amber nudity, he wanted to drop to his knees and worship her. With his tongue, with his lips—

She must have read his intention, because she jerked her head at him. "Oh no, big guy. Your turn."

The determination in her voice made him harden even further. He gave a strangled laugh. "Is that your 'managing your staff' voice?"

"I told you I was good at my job. Off with that shirt. We'll get to your staff in a minute."

"At your service."

He ripped off his T-shirt and tossed it on one of the window seats.

NITA GULPED, TORN between wondering what she'd gotten herself into and thanking the universe for sending this man to Santa Lucia. Good grief, he was built. Everywhere she looked, she saw hard ridges of sculpted muscle. She saw a lean waist with not a speck of flab, mighty shoulders rippling with restrained power. The men she had known in L.A. worked out, but this was a different kind of strength, the kind that tested itself against heavy equipment and fallen debris every day. And won.

She released a soft sigh, and along with it her last remaining qualms. Not that she had any doubts. She'd left those somewhere along the road to the lighthouse, or maybe she'd left them in the Knit, Purl, and Tea, when the sight of him scowling in that crazy apron had made her heart burst open.

Okay, so this was probably going nowhere. Who cared? Jeb was sexy, caring, totally hot, and he made her laugh. After the last two years, didn't she deserve some fun? Fun of the mind-blowingly-orgasmic variety? Didn't she deserve a little sexual healing?

"Pants," she told him.

Raising an eyebrow at her, he obeyed, unbuttoning his jeans and sliding them down, the muscles of his arms flexing as he bent, then straightened again. He kicked away his jeans and boxers, then stood naked before her in nothing but wind-mussed hair and a spectacular erection.

Good God. She put a hand to her head, feeling slightly faint. It wasn't a matter of size, though he did just fine in that sense. It was about *arousal*. He was so male, so hard, so potent, it was nearly too much for her system. For two years, everything had been sadness and doctors and anxiety and abandonment.

Now this. *Him.*

Wanting her.

Very badly, if that stiff penis was any indication.

Everything female within her responded. Suddenly she felt like a goddess, or a siren. She dropped her hand to her side, reveling in the way he feasted his eyes on her body. Her nipples hardened under his stare. She resisted the urge to hide that telltale sign, especially when she saw what it did to his erection.

She was a woman wanting a man. What was wrong with that? Nothing, her body told her. Nothing at all.

When his eyes met hers, she gave him a smile that would have been a purr, if she were a cat.

"Come here," he said roughly. "Before I lose my mind."

She stepped forward, into his arms, and into a world of heat and need and clenched muscles and bare skin. Her nipples hardened to an ache against the hard surface of his chest. She rubbed against him, delighting in the slight friction of the furry patch of hair.

He ran his hands down her back until he reached her ass, then yanked her against him. She groaned, going weak in the knees at the feel of his hot shaft pressing into her pelvis and belly. His arms vibrated like twin steel cables.

"Remember how I mentioned those five years?" His voice came in a painfully strangled shadow of its normal deep self.

"Yes," she whispered.

"I'm feeling every one of them right now. I don't know if I'll be able to go slow, Nita. I want you more than you'll ever know."

"No slow." She put her mouth to his ear. "Take me. Right now. We'll go slow later."

"In a minute." He reached down between them, between her legs, and tenderly touched her wet cleft. She gave a little cry as sensation soared through her. Closing her eyes, she tilted her head back to give herself fully to the glory of it. Oh, how he touched her, exploring her body with his full attention, his entire being tuned to her reactions. And she didn't hide them. She let him see every jolt of pleasure, every new shiver of happiness, every uptick in the need that tightened her body. He pushed her legs apart with his knee, and that movement alone gave her a shock of desire.

The feel of his strong thigh separating her legs, the sense of power in the hand that touched her so deliberately, the way he supported her with his other arm—everything built until she couldn't hold back her need. She let out little whimpers of urgency—*there, oh God, please, yes, more, oh my God don't stop*—pushing her mound against his hand. But he was so strong, he wouldn't let her control the contact. Instead he kept working his magic, stoking the fire until it burst into full, glorious life, sparks filling every corner of her mind with brilliant joy.

And then, only then, when she'd ridden the last current of that wild orgasm, he donned a condom, lifted her up, wrapped her legs around his hips, carried her to the wall and speared her.

She felt the impact all the way down to her toes—tingling waves of obliterating pleasure. Unbelievably, she came again, nearly instantly, though maybe she'd never really stopped. With his big hands supporting her ass, he corkscrewed into her with a couple of slow, intense strokes, then let all restraint go. With a deep-chested groan, he threw his head back and surrendered to his own orgasm. The sight of him, this powerful man shaking from his release, holding her as if he never wanted to stop, made a tear leak down her cheek.

Or maybe that was just the aftereffect of the most sorely needed orgasm of all time.

Seriously, she felt like a new woman. As if she could sing an opera, or dance on the Empire State Building. She still had her arms around him, and could feel his shuddering breaths.

"Thank you," he whispered in her ear. "Thank you. You have no idea." He let her slide down his body until she was back on her feet.

"You're wrong," she told him. "I know just how you

feel." Sexual healing, that's what this was. Definitely for her, maybe for him too. Maybe his confidence had taken a hit the same way hers had. "That was incredible." She kissed his chest tenderly, feeling it rise and fall. "Those five years don't show at all."

He laughed, his tiger-gold eyes bright as pennies. "Oh, they show, all right. I could make love to you again right now. Can you make up for five years in a few days?"

A shadow dimmed her joy. Of course. He'd be leaving soon. In her ecstatic afterglow, she'd forgotten that detail. *That's all right*, she told herself. *Take the sexual healing and enjoy. Nothing lasts forever.*

The faint blare of the ferry's horn interrupted her thoughts. "We'd better run. People get testy if you leave your groceries just sitting on the wharf. Here."

She tossed him his boxers and jeans, and stepped into her sundress. He pulled on his T-shirt, his muscles bunching. She took a moment to appreciate his solid, powerful build, and thought of how straightforward he'd been in every conversation they'd had. Maybe this was just sexual healing, but no matter what, she could trust this man. He wouldn't lie to her. He wouldn't pretend something he didn't feel, then run for cover when things got real.

With his honesty, his integrity, his dry sense of humor, and his incredible love making, he was definitely someone she could fall in love with. She'd have to make completely, absolutely sure she didn't. Another heartbreak would shatter her.

When they reached the wharf, all thoughts of love fled

at the sight that greeted them. A confused throng of reporters, camera people, and other members of the media milled around the dock. Camera equipment filled the cargo shed.

The senator's secret location wasn't a secret anymore.

Chapter Seven

THE ENCHANTED GARDEN was under siege. The sidewalk out front bristled with tripods and cameras. Reporters paced back and forth, cell phones in one hand, coffee cups in the other. When the ladies arrived for their tea, Jeb had to push his way through the crowd and personally escort them inside.

Spotting a business opportunity, Angie gave in and began brewing coffee for the hordes and charging an outrageous five dollars a cup. In Jeb's opinion, it should have been ten considering the amount of aggravation the press provoked. But he was happy about the coffee.

Inside the inn, things were just as crazy as outside. The senator ranted and roared, until Nita managed to convince him that it was inevitable word would get out. Then he slammed the door to his room and told everyone he needed some time alone.

No one minded giving him that.

As soon as the reporters had seen Nita, they'd begun pestering her for a statement. Jeb had to admire how she handled the situation, keeping her cool and her manners, and maintaining a steady sense of humor. It was clear that the reporters respected her, and even though she kept telling them she'd have something for them shortly, they still peppered her with questions.

Seeing the lines of stress reappear on her face, he longed to whisk her away somewhere private. Somewhere they could be alone, and he could work on that slow love-making he'd promised her.

It stunned him how much he wanted her. How much he wanted to be close to her. He didn't even know her, not really. And yet she'd given him something precious. When she'd let him into her confidence, she'd given him a piece of herself. It created a bond between them that felt very significant. He wanted more—he wanted to talk more, touch more, laugh more.

But his first responsibility was to Brody, and that meant getting Melissa the hell away from this madness. Which meant he'd have to leave the island, and Nita, as soon as possible.

He tapped on Melissa's door, then entered at her distracted "come in." She was standing in front of her dresser, her body angled sideways so she could reach her laptop, which was balanced on top of some books. One hand was typing, the other rubbing her lower back.

"Melissa, that doesn't look comfortable," he said in alarm.

"It's fine. I'm almost done."

"I think we should try to catch the afternoon ferry out."

"Uh-huh." With both hands on her keyboard, she clicked furiously.

"How about if I pack your things while you wrap up your story."

"Uh-huh."

He was pretty sure she hadn't heard him, but decided to proceed anyway. Spotting her suitcase in the corner, he dragged it out and set it on the bed.

"What are you doing?"

"Packing." He gave her a brief glance, unsurprised to see her green eyes throwing sparks at him.

"I can't leave yet. The senator wants to do another interview. If I leave, he'll wind up talking to one of those other billion reporters out there. I'll lose my entire exclusive."

"But if you leave now, you can get back to San Gabriel and get your story on the air first."

"It won't work that way. The senator wants to talk. Those reporters out there are just as good as I am. Probably better. And they work for national news organizations. Unless I'm right here under his nose, he'll decide it makes more sense to talk to one of them. I can't leave."

He straightened up and studied her for a long moment. "How are you feeling?"

"Fine. The same as before they showed up. Really, Jeb, I appreciate it. I admit I've had my hormonal moments, but this isn't one of them."

He deliberated. His main concern was her health. If she felt fine, there was no reason to whisk her away. Not that he could, if she didn't want to go. "Will you promise to tell me if you feel anything unusual? The slightest little twinge or pain or any warning sign whatsoever?"

Her expression softened into a warm smile. "You're really a good guy, aren't you?'

He shrugged. "I don't know about that, but when I tell someone I'm going to do something, I do it. And even if I hadn't told Brody I'd keep an eye on you, you're eight months pregnant and I'm an EMT, so I'd be paying attention anyway. I checked around, and the only doctor on this island is seventy-two years old. Your go-to guys are the volunteer firefighters, but from what I'm hearing, there might be some holes in their training. In serious cases, your options are a Medevac or a fire boat that takes an hour to get out here. I'm your guy, Melissa. I hope you're okay with that."

"I am," she said promptly. "Believe me, I don't want anything to harm the baby. If I was worried, I'd tell you."

"And if I feel strongly that for the sake of your health, and that of the baby, we should leave? What then?"

"I'll consider it."

He pinned her with a narrow stare until she bowed her head.

"I'll do what you say. Since you're an EMT. And Brody trusts you. And the most important thing is the baby."

"Thank you."

NITA WATCHED FROM the doorway, clutching her cell phone, feeling as if her heart was cracking open. Even though she had Brody on the line waiting to talk to Melissa, she couldn't bring herself to interrupt their conversation. Jeb wasn't even with Melissa, and he was more concerned about her baby than Bradford had been about his own. Would things have been different if someone like Jeb had been by her side? She would have still lost the baby, of course, but would she have completely broken down if she'd had someone as steady and caring as Jeb going through it with her?

She shook off that useless train of thought. The past was the past, and Jeb was leaving as soon as he could convince Melissa to go. After a quick knock on the door, she walked in and handed her phone to Melissa.

"It's Brody. He's been trying to reach both of you, and he's going crazy."

Melissa took the phone and walked a few steps away to speak quietly into it.

Jeb dug his cell from his pocket and frowned at it. "No service."

"Apparently one of the towers is temporarily down. Angie says it happens sometimes, especially when the storms hit."

He glanced out the window, where clouds were beginning to skim across the sky. "Doesn't look too bad out there."

"Brody said he's been watching the Weather Channel and a big storm system has changed direction. It's heading toward us instead of out to sea."

His forehead creased with worry. "I don't like that. I don't like that at all."

"Well, it's a couple of days out. And it might peter out before then, or change direction again. I told Brody not to worry too much, but I should have saved my breath."

He gave a ghost of a smile. "He's going to worry for the next eighteen years. At least. So, how's the hungry mob out there?"

"They're not happy with me. They think I'm stone-walling. One of them tried to disguise himself as a pizza delivery guy. As if I don't recognize every single one of them."

"Are they bothering you? You tell me, and I'll kick their asses. One or all of them." The intensity in his voice sparked a thrill deep in her belly.

"I can handle them." It was her job. The one thing so far she hadn't failed at.

"I know you can. But if you need a little extra muscle, you call on me. Hear?" He looked dangerous, with that scowl emphasizing the severe planes of his face. His hands were stuck in his back pockets, which made his T-shirt strain against the muscles of his chest. Not so long ago, she'd been tracing those very muscles with her tongue.

"I hear."

She wanted to throw herself at him. Get caught up in his strong arms and let the rest of the world fade to static.

He must have picked up on her mood, because his eyes changed, darkened with knee-melting desire. He lowered his voice until it was nearly inaudible. "What are you doing later?"

She managed a shrug.

"I'll find you. I'm going to take Charlie up on his invitation, no matter what the fire chief says. I want to scope out the fire department and see just how ill-prepared they are. With Melissa determined to stay, and a storm coming, I want to know what I'm dealing with. I won't be long."

"I'll see you later."

"Yes, you will." With a scorching look, he strode out the door.

Melissa hung up with Brody and turned to Nita. As soon as she caught sight of Nita's expression, she broke into a huge smile. "Oh my. You're smitten."

"I'm not—oh, crap."

JEB SPENT ABOUT an hour chatting with the Santa Lucia volunteer firefighters. The fire chief, the only actual paid staff member, wasn't around. Apparently that wasn't unusual. The guys were young, eager, lively, and sadly disorganized. One problem was that people kept quitting out of frustration, which meant that the crew was always getting used to new members. Half-trained volunteers were training the new recruits, and misinformation was getting amplified. The captain in him longed to take them in hand and apply some proper discipline to the station. But it wasn't his business, and considering he'd been warned off by the chief himself, unwise.

One thing was for certain. If something happened with Melissa, he wouldn't trust the San-L fire department to handle the situation. A fire, sure. A car accident, maybe. Brody's baby—absolutely not.

Charlie offered him a fish burger and a ride back to the Enchanted Garden, which he accepted. The kid's jaw dropped at the sight of the media circus still camped out on the sidewalk. Persistent, he'd give them that. It was getting dark, but they weren't budging.

"Should we come up with a crowd control contingency plan?" Charlie asked Brody in awe.

"Couldn't hurt," Jeb said. "Nice initiative."

Beaming, the firefighter drove off while Jeb, hands shoved into his pockets, surveyed the Enchanted Garden.

Light glowed from within the cozy inn, with its corner turret and gingerbread trim. The turret reminded him of the lighthouse, which inspired all kinds of naughty thoughts about Nita Moreno.

And suddenly he wanted her desperately. This situation must be a nightmare for her. Over the past couple of days, he'd seen her relax, seen the bright-eyed woman he remembered from the wedding return. But now her tension was back, no matter how much she claimed the reporters didn't bother her.

He had some thoughts about how to relieve that tension.

He went through the side entrance, locking it behind him in case any overly dedicated reporters tried to follow him. The door let onto the kitchen, where the lights were out and everything was in place. The copper frying pans gleamed in the glow of the pilot light. The refrigerator hummed. It really was a lovely, comforting spot, despite the ruffle overload. He cocked his head, listening for other signs of life. Maybe the senator and Melissa were still working. Maybe he could get Nita alone and ravage her senseless.

That pleasant vision shimmered to life as Nita walked in, carrying an armful of teacups. Her hair was loose, the dark waves tumbling over her shoulders. Over the sundress—which was burned into his brain—she wore a fuzzy white sweater. She started at the sight of him, and the teacups rattled. With a quick movement, he rescued one and stabilized the others. When the cups were safely stowed on the counter, he put his hands on her shoulders and turned her to face him.

Yep, sure enough, that anxious look was back. Apparently his mighty cock hadn't chased it away for good.

Yet.

Smiling at his own idiocy, he smoothed his hands down her arms, until he held her hands. "How are you doing?" He asked her softly.

"Oh, fabulous. The senator's blaming me for the media circus. He's threatening to take it out on Melissa by scrapping her exclusive. The fire chief is threatening to fine me for clogging the sidewalk. Angie's channeling Bette Davis and ordering me around like a scullery maid. And Melissa keeps snapping at me. Maybe she blames me too."

"Aw, honey." The word slipped from his lips before he even thought about it. It felt completely natural, but it made Nita's eyes widen.

"And . . ." she gave a goofy smile. "I missed you."

"I've only been gone a couple of hours."

"I know."

That was it. With provocation like that, who could blame him for what he did next? He bent down, scooped her into his arms, and strode into the hallway. She felt wonderful against him, warm and silky, her hair sliding across his arm. "I figured something out while I was standing out in the dark, scoping out this joint."

"What?" She sounded breathless, but he liked the way she clung to his neck.

"You got the tower room, didn't you? Like a princess waiting for her prince."

"Not true! I mean, yes, Angie put me in the tower room. She can't handle the stairs anymore. But the rest of it is ridiculous."

"Are you so sure?"

Taking the stairs two at a time, still holding her in his arms, he climbed to the top floor. By the time he reached the landing outside the tower room door, he was panting. "Maybe you need a prince who's in better shape," he gasped, setting her down.

"That's impossible. Who else could have carried me up three flights of stairs?"

A couple of the San Gabriel firefighters came to mind, Vader Brown in particular. But he chose not to mention that.

"Now get in here before you have a heart attack." She opened the door for him. Staggering inside, he collapsed on the big bed, which was scattered with ruffled little pillows. The room had curved windows on three sides, with a view of tree tops and clouds. Right now, the trees were moving restlessly in the wind. The crescent moon kept emerging and disappearing behind the racing mass of clouds.

"Any word on the forecast?" He asked Nita. She was prowling toward the bed—there was no other word for it. Slinky and determined as a panther, she climbed onto the bed, straddled him and ran her fingers under the waistband of his jeans.

"Yes. The forecast is for horny."

"Accurate so far."

"They're calling for lots of nakedness." She unbuttoned his fly, which bulged from the pressure of his rising erection.

"Those naughty weather people. Are we on 'Stormwatch' yet?" The Southern California news stations were infamous for their weather freakouts.

"We're on 'Sexwatch.'" She lifted her dress and eased herself against his groin. He lifted his hips and pushed his jeans out of the way. His cock was trying to burst out of the opening in his boxers. When he tried to fix it, she shoved his hands away and did it herself, maneuvering his shorts off his shaft and down to his thighs.

"I hope there's more than watching involved," he gasped.

She licked her lips and rocked her soft wetness against his penis. Maybe he'd died and this was heaven, this little tower room and this amazing woman.

Then she stilled for a moment. "I don't have a condom."

"Married for eighteen years, sex-free for the past five. You don't have to worry about me."

"And they tested me up the wazoo in the hospital. Literally. If a wazoo is what I think it is."

The sultry heat in her eyes didn't lessen a bit at her mention of the hospital. That had to be progress. But still . . . "Do you think you could stop talking now? I'm trying to concentrate."

"On what?"

"Fucking your brains out." Finding her opening, he thrust into her, pleasure streaking from the base of his cock, up his spine, and into his brain. "Holy Mother of God, that's good, Nita."

Her head was tilted back, her glorious hair swaying with the motion of her body. He put his hands on the front of her little sundress. "How important is this dress?"

"Three dollars at a thrift store," she gasped. "Has a stain on the back."

He ripped it open. The buttons landed on the floor in a flurry of dull clunks. She was naked underneath the dress—sleekly, wonderfully naked. He flicked his thumbs across her nipples, lightly, the way he'd already figured out she liked.

"Oh Jeb," she breathed softly, the sound going right to his already engorged cock. He pumped into her, slow and sure and rhythmic, feasting his eyes on her. If he was the drum, pounding out a steady beat, she was the lead singer, every sensual movement of her body like a melody made into flesh. With every one of her sexy little shudders, she inflamed him even more, until all he knew was the blood thundering in his ears.

He gripped her soft hips, felt them tremble. She was

making a keening little moan with every one of his up-thrusts. He loved that sound. Loved knowing how turned on she was, how much pleasure he was giving her. He loved the way she threw herself into their lovemaking, the way all her sadness vanished when they were in bed.

He wanted to live and die here, buried inside her. The intensity of the feeling shocked him.

And then the urgent drumbeat picked up speed, thundered through his veins, driving him on and on, up and up, into her body, into that soft, clenching heat. Her inner muscles tightened around him. She called out his name in a wild voice. And he splintered into a million shards of glory.

Chapter Eight

SINCE HER FIRST night here, Nita had imagined making love in this perfect little turret room. From the first moment, the room had felt like a bubble of serenity, almost like a snow globe, a safe place where nothing could hurt her. But she'd never pictured anything as raw and wild as what she'd just experienced with Jeb Stone.

She lay next to him, catching her breath, basking in the heat that radiated from his solid body. The sound of his jagged breathing filled the quiet room. She listened as his breath returned to normal. The sweat began to cool on both of their bodies. She huddled close to him, felt his strong arm come around her. And the question that had been simmering in her mind bubbled over.

"What was it like before the last five years?"

"What?"

Yes, she had to admit, it was a confusing question. "You and your ex stopped having sex five years ago. But what was your relationship like before then? Because you're . . . well . . ." How could she put this? "You're a fantastic lover."

Scalding heat washed across her face. That wasn't exactly what she meant to say, though it was true.

"What I mean is, you seem very sexual."

He lolled his head to the side and cast her an amused glance. "Very sexual, huh? I think I'll take that as a compliment. Unless you're wondering if my insatiable need for sex drove my wife away."

"Of course I didn't mean that." The thought flitted through her mind that if she was with Jeb, she'd be even more insatiable than he was. "I'm just asking inappropriately personal questions."

"Honey. We're naked in bed. How could anything be inappropriate?" He laid his big warm hand on her stomach. She felt the heat travel through to her spine. Tendrils of desire meandered to her sex. The man did something to her, something she wasn't completely prepared for.

"So I can ask you anything?"

"You might have noticed that I'm a big believer in honesty. For better or worse."

"Is your wife gay?" As soon as she said it, she clapped one hand over her mouth, then added the other on top of that one. Maybe two hands would be able to bring back that blurted question.

Peering up at him, she saw it was not to be. He'd heard the question, all right. His tiger eyes glittered.

"Melissa," he hissed grimly.

"Don't blame her! I was curious."

With a sudden movement, he flipped her onto her back and braced himself over her, the weight of his body pinning her to the bed. He looked and felt so powerful, looming over her. "You want the story?" He asked in a low voice. "Or did Melissa tell you all you need to know? Did she give a full report to her friendly neighborhood press agent?"

She pushed at his chest, which was more or less like pushing at a cement wall. But he relented and withdrew enough so she could sit up. "That's horribly unfair, Jeb. I'm not a press agent right now. I'm a woman in bed with a man. And I couldn't help wondering about you and Belinda."

He ran his hand through his hair, his muscles flexing. She hated that she'd upset him.

"Melissa shared her private speculations, and told me that's what they were. She also told me to keep them private, and instead I just blurted it out to you. So I'm to blame, not her."

He rolled away from her, stretching out on his back, and threw his forearm across his eyes. "No blame. It's okay. I just haven't faced this situation before. Usually it's enough to say, 'I'm amicably divorced.'"

"It is enough. It's fine," Nita said quickly. "You don't have to explain anything to me. I'm sorry I brought it up."

"No. Don't be sorry. I'm not. It's a part of me. If you want me, this goes with the package."

Wild butterflies took flight in Nita's stomach. *If she wanted him?* What was he offering? Could he possibly be thinking beyond the next few days? "I want you," she said softly, choosing not to think about the many possible meanings of that statement. "I want to hear. I want to know."

He took a deep breath, his chest rising and falling. "I don't know if I would say Belinda's 'gay'. I'd say she loves sex, and she loves women, and she loves me. But she loves women more. She's with a woman now. In Thailand."

"So . . ." Nita shook her head in confusion. "She's not a lesbian? Or she sometimes is?"

"You'd have to know Belinda to understand. That's why I don't go by labels anymore. Everyone's unique. I've known Belinda since we were kids. We both came from very repressed families. Very rigid, very strict, especially about sexuality. I rebelled early on. I partied a lot. But it was easier for me to sow my wild oats than it was for her. I was her first attempt at stepping outside the line, and when we got pregnant, of course we had to marry."

"Of course?"

"We cared about each other and we both wanted a family. It was a no-brainer. We had Alison. Things were good. The first years with Alison we were scrambling. I was trying to get my firefighting career going, she was always sleep-deprived. When things settled down, we remembered what brought us together in the first place." He shot her a sidelong glance, his tiger eyes picking up a spark from the moon. "Sex."

Nita gulped. Well, she'd asked for the whole story.

"We started going wild in the bedroom. Belinda wanted to try everything. We were married, so it was okay in her mind. She finally got her chance to sow those oats. Being a red-blooded young man, I didn't mind. But the more time went on, the more it became obvious that Belinda was more excited about other women than anything else."

Nita listened in growing astonishment. What was missing from this speech? It took her a minute to put her finger on it. Oh yeah. *Bitterness.* "And that was okay with you? That she preferred women?"

A muscle in his jaw flexed. His body, so snug against hers, tensed.

"I won't lie. I had some rough moments. But I got through it. I love Belinda, but she was always a handful. She'd probably say the same about me. We sort of . . . raised each other. Saw each other through our wild times. We were kids when we got married, we didn't know what the hell we were doing. But we took care of each other, and managed to put our daughter first. Well, mostly. Belinda probably knew ten years ago that she didn't want to be married anymore, but she stuck it out. I don't blame her for anything. And I'll always love her. She's my family. Whatever she is or isn't, I still love her. Even if it doesn't fit into what I thought my life would be."

Nita swallowed hard. Was he saying that he was still in love with his ex-wife? Even though she'd switched to the other team? Not that she had a right to ask. This thing between her and Jeb was . . . well, it wasn't anything. A few days of sexual bliss that might end at any moment.

But she couldn't help herself. She had to know. They were naked in bed, and he'd said nothing was too personal. She inhaled a deep breath. "You still love her?"

"Of course I do."

Her stomach sank like a falling elevator. "Oh."

He glanced at her sharply, then raised himself on one elbow. "You goose. You think I'm pining after my runaway, lesbian ex-wife? No. I love Belinda because I grew up with her, I married her, she's Alison's mother, and I know her inside out. But we don't love each other like *that*. She's like a . . . not a sister, exactly. She's part of me. But she's not my future."

The word "future" trembled in the air. A future was exactly what they didn't have. Especially now that she knew about his marriage. Nita couldn't imagine him waltzing from a long, complicated relationship like his marriage to Belinda into something new. He needed to enjoy his freedom. Remember the joys of sex. Reconnect with the side of him that had tried all those wild things with Belinda.

Jealousy percolated through her like an overflowing coffee pot. She couldn't help it. How could an uptight, driven press secretary ever compete with the memory of the adventurous Belinda, who also happened to be the mother of his child?

A sense of bleakness made her drop her head to her pillow. She'd let herself get too involved, too quickly. Sexual healing was one thing; getting your heart broken was another. And these days, her heart was too fragile to risk.

A finger tapped gently on her forehead. "What's going on in there? What wheels are turning?"

"Nothing."

"Not buying that. You've got to be thinking something. If you're rewriting the senator's statement, we're going to have a problem."

She snorted into her pillow.

"Have I blown your mind? Are you figuring out how to tell me to get lost?" Despite the humor in his voice, she sensed it wasn't an easy question for him to ask.

Since he'd been so open with her, she couldn't lie to him. "No. Not that. Did you ever ... I don't know ... doubt yourself? When she stopped wanting sex?"

He stayed silent for a long moment. Wind rustled against the windows. "Maybe a little. But only a little. I tried not to take it personally. That's who she is. And she enjoyed sex with me plenty over the years. I'm ... well, confident in that arena."

As well he should be, she thought. The man was a package of dynamite wrapped up in a devastating body. He was magnetic, magical, forceful. Not only that, he paid attention. He'd already figured out what pleased her, and did those things until she was thoroughly satisfied. He was, easily, the best lover she'd ever had.

Whereas she had failed at being a woman. Failed to keep Bradford. Failed to carry her baby.

There was only one thing to do. Retreat, before the damage to her heart grew even worse.

AN UNPLEASANT BANGING woke Nita from vaguely disturbing dreams about tsunamis and sand castles.

"Nita! Nita Moreno!"

Ugh, it was the senator's deep, carrying voice, the voice that didn't even need a microphone to speak to a crowd of thousands. When he called for her in that angry tone, it meant that he'd screwed something up and needed her right away. That tone meant stress, panic, adrenaline.

She sat up with a jolt, horrified at the thought of her boss catching her in bed with a man.

Except there was no man in her bed.

Right. She'd feigned exhaustion, then dropped off to sleep. Then she'd woken up when he'd tried to tiptoe out of the room. Panicked at the thought of never getting to make love with him again, she'd lured him back to bed, where they'd explored every inch of each other's bodies and she'd come twice more, once under the skillful stroking of his tongue, once at the touch of his fingers.

He was *too* skillful. It made her nervous. They'd fallen asleep again, and he must have left sometime after that.

Thank goodness he had, because the senator was in a mood.

"This statement is *shite*," he growled as soon as she threw on a robe and opened the door.

"It's perfect."

He waved the pages in the air, then violently crumpled them in a ball and tossed them on the floor. Then he stomped on them.

"You do realize that's just one copy," she said dryly. "The original's on my computer."

"I can't go out there and say those words."

"Which ones? 'I'm sorry?'"

He stormed to the window. "I'm a state senator. *A sen-*

ator! Apology is a sign of weakness. Can't I just regret if someone was offended?"

"That's not going to cut it."

"It's my private life! I'll go as far as apologizing if someone was offended, but that's all."

"Very gracious of you. I'm sure your constituents will appreciate that." Nita felt a slow rise of disgust. Did everything have to be a word game? What would Jeb do in this situation? He was a fire captain. Would he think apologizing made him "weak"?

"Don't get rude with me. Now rewrite that garbage statement and book me a helicopter. I want off this island."

A spitting rain, pushed by gusts of wind, clattered against the windows. Nita folded her arms over her chest, pulling her robe tighter around her. "No."

"*What?*"

"The statement is fine. It's what you need to say. Anything less and you'll be crucified. I'm not changing it."

"Damn it, Nita. You work for me. That means you do what I tell you."

"I'm not your servant." She was starting to tremble. "I'm your press secretary. You hired me for my expertise."

"I hired you for your demographic profile," he snapped. "Now fix the statement."

A chill rippled through her, rooted her to the floor. He'd hired her because her family was Mexican? Was that it? The sum total of five years of hard work and brutal hours? Did he really think so little of her? The icy cold feeling transformed into hot, molten rage. Red spots danced before her eyes. "Get out of my room."

"Get me a new statement."

"No. I'm never writing another word for you. I quit."

His jaw fell open. Scarlet flashed across his genial, lying face. "No, you don't."

"Oh, I do. Do whatever you want to your statement. Whatever you want to your career. It has nothing to do with me anymore. Now get out of my room before I call the cops on you."

She didn't even know if Santa Lucia had cops, but she could always call on Jeb.

"I don't accept your resignation."

"It's not a resignation. It's a quitting." She clenched her fists. Why didn't he leave? He was still standing by the window, staring at her as if she were a two-headed calf. Or a *chupacabra*, to use a reference from her "demographic profile."

The thought made her fury beat louder, the blood singing in her ears. She couldn't stand to be in the room with him for another second. Cinching the belt of her robe tight, she stalked toward the door. "If you aren't leaving, I will. Good day, and goodbye."

Flinging the door open, she burst onto the landing and took a deep gulp of air that was untainted by the senator's presence. What a fool she'd been to pour her heart and soul into working for him, when it meant nothing to him. All this time, had he seen her as a checkmark on a quota form? Had he ever appreciated her skill?

He didn't deserve her. A feeling of power swept through her. God, it felt good to quit. Good to claim her own life. She should have done it long ago. She should have done it when . . . a hiccup of a sob broke out . . . when he'd given her a grand total of a week off to recover from the miscarriage. Which she'd told him was an allergic reaction to nuts. That's how afraid she'd been to lose her precious job.

Well, it was gone now. No baby. No boyfriend. No job. She was three for three.

Chapter Nine

"I KNOW ABOUT the storm," Jeb told Brody over the phone. They must have gotten the tower back up, because he finally had cell service again. "Have you forgotten that I'm here, and I can look outside and see the weather?"

"What does it look like?"

He lifted the hem of one of the Knit, Purl, and Tea's lacy curtains. A wash of gray greeted him, as if the bed and breakfast was going through a car wash. "Wet. Windy."

"Well, I don't like it. I want Melissa home. Now."

Jeb sighed. Of course he understood Brody's fear, but what did the man think he could do? "She's trying to protect her story. As soon as the press leaves, she will too."

"I don't want my baby's life hinging on the fucking press," Brody growled. "I hate the press."

"Your wife's a reporter."

"Don't remind me. Jeb, I think I'd better come out

there. I should be able to leave tonight or tomorrow morning. She'll be fine until then, right?"

"I'll make sure of it."

"I owe you, Stone." He gave a dry laugh. "Anything except my first born child."

"A joke. That's good. Try to relax, will you?"

Brody didn't answer. Jeb knew he was pacing, because there wasn't much else he could do at this point, from that distance. Maybe the man needed a distraction.

"Got a question for you."

"Shoot."

He gave a quick glance around the deserted breakfast room. "How long did it take before you knew you and Melissa would end up together?"

"You met someone."

"Not an answer."

"I don't have a solid answer. It was a wild ride and I never knew what was around the next corner. Are we talking about Melissa's friend Nita?"

Jeb's jaw shifted from side to side. Brody knew Belinda, of course. But he didn't know *everything* about Belinda. Maybe he wouldn't support the idea of a new woman in Jeb's life. "Yeah," he said finally.

"Uh-huh."

"That's your word of wisdom? Uh-huh? Come on, Brody, I know you're famous for your cryptic comments, but you can give me a little more than 'uh-huh.'"

"Maybe that's all you need."

Jeb's irritation grew. The firehouse crew had lots of fun trying to decipher Brody's statements. He was legendary for them, as well as for the number of lives he'd saved. San Gabriel Station 1 was a highly sought after assignment because of Brody. But that didn't give him the right to drive Jeb crazy. "Care to explain?"

"Look, Jeb. You pull a structure fire. The whole house is one big bonfire. Everyone's saying no one's left inside. But you see something move at a window, something that looks like a hand waving. Then it's gone. No one else saw it. Maybe you imagined it. Logic says it was probably your eyes playing tricks with you. Your gut instinct says someone's in there. What do you do?"

"I get a ladder up to that window and go in."

"There you go."

"What? What are you talking about?" But Brody had covered the mouthpiece of the phone and was saying something to Danielle, their adopted daughter.

"Gotta go, Stone. Do as I said, and you'll be fine."

"But—" He was speaking to empty air.

Empty except for the rattling of the windowpanes. Outside, a white lawn chair tumbled across the garden. Someone lost a red umbrella, which went somersaulting down the street. The storm was on the rise.

Charlie, wearing orange rubber rain gear, burst through the front door, followed by a vicious swirl of wind. Panting, he pushed his dripping rain hat back on his head. "I have . . . to secure my boat."

"Your boat?"

"Yeah. When I'm not a volunteer fireman, I'm a fisherman."

"Gotcha. Better get moving; it's getting nasty out there."

"That's what I came to tell you. The *Danny B.* is suspending service after this afternoon's run. If you don't make that boat, there might not be another chance for a while."

Jeb stiffened in alarm. Brody would be furious if Melissa got stranded by the storm. He had to get her on the boat.

Charlie thrust a pager into Jeb's hand. "Take this. Beep me if you need anything."

"You're a good man, Charlie Scott."

Charlie saluted, flinging drops of water across the lace curtains. Just as he retreated out the front door, rapid footsteps sounded in the corridor. Jeb swung around as Nita flew into the breakfast room, still in her bathrobe. Her eyes looked enormous and her hair rioted loose and wild down her back.

He met her halfway across the room and caught her in his arms. "What's the matter?"

"Nothing. Everything's great. Where's Angie? Where's Melissa?"

"Melissa's in her room, wrapping things up. I just got the news that the last ferry's this afternoon. I want her on that boat."

"I'll help her pack." She tried to pull herself out of his grasp, but he held her tight.

"Wait. Don't rush off yet. Tell me what's wrong."

"*Nothing's wrong.* Well, I quit my job." Her hand flew to her mouth. She looked astonished by her revelation.

"Congratulations."

"Huh?" Two little lines appeared between her eyebrows. He longed to smooth them away.

"You could use a break," he said.

"A break." She leaned back in the circle of his arms and tilted her head to look at him. "Is that what I need?"

"I think it's helping already. You aren't doing that thing you do with your cheek."

She touched her own cheek. "You noticed that?"

"Of course. It's hard to miss."

"No one ever noticed before. Not even Bradford."

"Really?" That seemed impossible to him. "You were doing it at the wedding."

"It's a stress reliever."

He brushed her wild hair away from her face. "May I suggest an alternative stress reliever?" A wolfish grin accompanied that offer. He felt like a wolf right now, a big bad wolf who could eat her alive.

She started to tremble in his arms. "I can't believe I quit my job. What am I going to do? Where am I going to go? What am I going to *be*?"

He ran one hand down her back in an attempt to soothe her, though it had the simultaneous effect of exciting him. "Whatever it is, I can't wait to see."

"Nita." A sharp voice spoke from the other side of the room. The senator stood poker-straight in the doorway, looking stiff and offended. "You've made a mistake. But I'll let you come back if you acknowledge it."

Nita tore herself out of Jeb's arms and faced off with the senator. "I suppose you'd like me to *apologize*. I suppose it's okay for a lowly peasant like me to apologize."

"Not necessary. I ordered a helicopter to get me off this island. It'll be here soon. I want a statement presented to the press before then. I want you to do it."

"But I don't work for you anymore."

"I'll take you back. I'm sure we can work a mutually agreeable arrangement."

"We can't," said Nita flatly. "I don't want to work for you anymore."

"But I bet you want Bradford Maddox back."

Jeb's breath stuttered in his chest. Nita went white. "What are you talking about?"

"I can get Maddox back for you. There's a bill pending that will make him a lot of money. So far I've refused to support it. But if I do, so will the rest of the Los Angeles area delegation. I'll do that for you. I'll even make sure he puts a ring on your finger. As long as you deal with this situation."

Jeb thought about how happy Nita had looked with Bradford. The man was wealthy. Powerful. At the reception, when Jeb had talked to her at the bar, she'd been nestled against Bradford like a dark-haired, beautiful kitten. Did she want her old boyfriend back? Did she want him back enough to condone what amounted to a bribe?

Nita had drawn further away from him. His hands itched to snatch her back, to show her that he was better for her than Bradford. Better than a guy who abandoned her when she was pregnant. He clenched them into tight fists to stop himself. This was her choice, not his. And he hadn't even told her his feelings. He didn't even *know* his feelings. But he wanted a chance to figure them out.

She took a step toward Stryker. Jeb's stomach plunged. She was going with the senator. Accepting his offer.

She took another step, then another. He closed his eyes, unable to bear the sight of Nita giving herself to people who didn't appreciate her.

A sharp sound ricocheted around the room. His eyes flew open in time to catch the tail end of a mighty slap across Senator Stryker's face.

"That's what I think of your disgusting offer. Don't ever suggest such a thing to me again."

Jeb's heart raced. Did that mean she didn't want Bradford anymore?

"Here's *my* offer," Nita continued. "I will craft a new statement. I'll even read it to the press. No charge. I don't want anything from you, ever again. The only thing I want is for you to take Melissa on the chopper with you. She needs to get off the island and the ferry would be miserable in this weather. Jeb too." Without looking at him, she gestured his direction. "He needs to stay close to Melissa."

"I don't know if there's room—"

"Make sure there is. I'll also expect a hefty donation to the Santa Lucia Fire Department for the crowd control they've been forced to deal with."

"What crowd control?"

"The volunteer firefighters have been swinging by to check on things," Jeb put in, his heart nearly leaping out of his chest. *She wasn't going back to Bradford.*

"Take it or leave it," Nita told the senator. "That's my final offer."

"Done. Have the statement ready in fifteen minutes."

NITA COULDN'T BELIEVE she'd just survived a standoff with the senator. Blindly, she turned to Jeb and threw herself into his arms. For some reason, that was the only place she wanted to be at that moment. He held her tight, his warmth surrounding her.

"Well done," he murmured. "Stryker didn't know who he was tangling with."

She couldn't stop shaking. She couldn't stop burrowing her head into his big body. "I have to get to work on that statement."

"I should pack, and let Melissa know we have a ride out of here, thanks to you."

A shudder passed through her, as it finally occurred to her what she'd just done. She'd arranged for Jeb's departure from her life.

It was for the best, of course. Not just because Melissa would be safer back on the mainland. But because *Nita* would be safer. No matter how much she gorged herself on this man's steady presence and skillful lovemaking, he wasn't for her. For those moments with him, she hadn't felt like a failure of a woman. She'd felt wonderful. Which meant it would be all the more crushing when it ended. Which it would.

Because he wasn't ready for the kind of relationship she wanted.

Maybe quitting her job had clarified her thoughts. Because suddenly it seemed perfectly clear that what she wanted was another chance to make a baby. She couldn't have her baby back, the baby on which she'd lavished four months of love and care. That baby was gone. Safe in the hands of the eternal. But another baby awaited, and that baby needed her. That baby needed a real father, too, not someone who offered nothing more than a monthly check.

Jeb had raised his daughter. He'd stayed married through some pretty challenging times. Now he was free. Why on earth would he want to do it all over again?

She drew away from him, wiped her eyes, and tightened the belt of her robe. "I'll be holed up with my computer. Come say goodbye before you guys go."

As BLOW-OFFS WENT, that one was pretty masterful, if you asked Jeb. Furious, he threw his things into his overnight bag, slung it over his shoulder, and crossed the narrow hallway to Melissa's room.

"Come in," she called.

She was just sliding her laptop into its sleeve. "Are we leaving?"

"Nita arranged seats for us on the senator's chopper."

"That Nita. Isn't she amazing? She's so good at organizing everything. And incredibly thoughtful. Don't you think?"

Jeb didn't trust himself to answer a question about Nita at the moment. Anyway, he had more pressing problems at the moment. He'd seen the wince Melissa had tried to hide as she zipped her laptop case. He spun Melissa's chair around so she faced him, then leaned down, fixing her with his captain's stare.

"What aren't you telling me?"

"What?"

"This isn't something to mess around with. Tell me exactly what's going on."

Something flickered in those deep green eyes. "You're so much like Brody it's eerie."

"Melissa," he warned.

"First, tell me if you like Nita."

He wanted to wring her neck. Not even hormones were an excuse for extortion. "Of course I like her," he ground out.

"Because she deserves to be liked. I know she comes across as someone who has it all together, but inside she's the softest, kindest, most generous—"

"*I like her.* You don't have to talk me into it. She did that all on her own."

A slow, delighted smile spread across her face. "You do like her," she murmured. "I'm so happy." Then she recoiled, hand on her belly. "Oh crap." She scrunched up her face. Jeb knelt next to her, rubbing her back in the way Belinda had appreciated.

"I've been having some pains," Melissa blurted. "They started last night. It's probably nothing. I mean, it's too early. And they're far apart. Probably Braxton-Hicks contractions, right? The false ones that come before the real ones?" She grabbed at his hand. "It's nothing to worry about, right?"

"Have you told Brody?"

"I don't want him to worry. I haven't told anyone except you. I called my OB-GYN and left a message, but I haven't heard back yet.

He straightened up. "I'm calling Brody."

"No! There's nothing he can do from there. He'll just go crazy. I don't want to do that to him."

"Then we're getting on that chopper and we'll call him from the mainland."

"Okay. Fine. If the senator really lets me on it. He's pretty ticked off."

"He'll let you," said Jeb grimly. He started imagining what he'd do to the senator if he objected. Those pleasant thoughts were interrupted by the sound of shouting outside.

Jeb hurried to the window and pulled back the ruffled curtain. The reporters were leaving en masse. Camera operators were throwing equipment into cases, reporters were running down the street. Nita hadn't even held her press conference yet, had she? He looked at his watch. Barely fifteen minutes had passed since he'd left her in the tea room. He nudged the window open. Water sprayed into the room. "What's going on?" He yelled to the disappearing crowd.

"The last ferry's here," someone answered. "It came early and it's leaving right away."

Jeb closed the window before the floor got too soaked. He turned back to Melissa. "It's a good thing Nita got us spots on the chopper."

"I guess it is. My stuff is packed. I'm ready to go." She

flinched again. Jeb was at her side in a second. She grabbed his hand and squeezed hard until the pain passed. "How do we get to the chopper?" She said with a gasp.

"I'll go find out. You're doing great, Melissa. Everything's going to be okay."

Empty words. But they'd better be true. He'd do everything in his power to make sure they were.

A steady thump-thumping sound made him look out the window again. A helicopter hovered directly overhead, its blades whipping rainwater in a wild pinwheel pattern. Peering out the window was the senator. He spotted Jeb and gave him the finger. Then the chopper lifted higher in the air, wheeled to the left, and headed toward the mainland.

So much for their ride off the island.

Chapter Ten

BY THE TIME Nita had indulged in a string of satisfying curses at Senator Stryker and the runaway reporters, she was ready to face Jeb in the empty tea room.

"Once the press left, Stryker must have figured our deal was pointless. What about the ferry?"

"It's probably gone by now. It's going to be packed anyway. I'm not comfortable with Melissa being crammed onto a ferryboat in a storm." He dragged a hand through his hair.

"Then we just stay here and ride it out?" A sneaky tendril of hope stole through her. Maybe she wouldn't have to say goodbye to Jeb yet.

"Where's Angie?"

"She went across the street to her friend's house. Apparently they have a storm knitting tradition."

Jeb lapsed into deep thought. Nita watched him, realizing that whatever decision he made, she would trust it.

"I'm going to call Brody and explain the situation. Can you check on Melissa?"

"Of course."

Nita hurried to Melissa's room and tapped on the door. "Melissa?" she called softly. No answer. She pushed the door open and stepped into an eerie stillness. *Oh my God. Something's wrong. Something happened.* She knew it with every cell of her body, every goose bump on her skin. Suddenly she felt as if she was drowning in terror. She couldn't move her feet, couldn't open her mouth. Images from the day she'd started bleeding cascaded through her mind. The absolute terror, the call to her doctor, the cab ride to the emergency room, the carefully neutral expressions of the nurses, the onrushing darkness.

"Melissa?" She managed to whisper.

"In here." Melissa's voice came from the bathroom.

She could make it to the bathroom. She had to, for Melissa's sake, and for her baby. Forcing one foot to lift, then the other, she moved jerkily across the bedroom to the tiny bathroom. When she pushed the door open, her first thought was that water had spilled on the floor. Melissa was standing over it. She looked up at Nita with an expression of complete astonishment.

"What the hell, I think my water broke! It shouldn't have done that. I still have another month to go."

That was bad, very bad. Sick fear grabbed at her throat. *Not Melissa. Not Melissa's baby.* She wanted to throw up. She felt as if a cloud of panicked hornets was swarming her brain.

"What do we do? What do we do?" What had she done

when she'd seen the blood? She'd called her doctor, then a cab. She turned blindly toward the door, then whirled back again. "I'll call 911. They'll send an ambulance. No, I have the Suburban. I can drive you to the hospital." She spun toward the door again.

"Nita." Melissa grabbed her upper arm and gave her a little shake. "It's going to be okay. Get Jeb. Just *get Jeb*. You hear me?"

Nita nodded, those two crucial words penetrating the fog of fear. *Get Jeb*. She could do that.

WHEN NITA RAN into the tearoom screaming for him, she was nearly incoherent, but Jeb got enough of the gist to spring into action.

"Could be premature rupture," he said. "Is she going into labor? Is she having regular contractions? Focus, Nita." He gripped her by the shoulders, willing her gaze to meet his. She took a deep, shuddering breath and passed a hand over her forehead.

"I'm sorry. I was just . . ."

"I know." He recognized a trauma flashback when he saw one. "Keep on breathing, you'll be okay." He ran through the options. Each of them required a functioning Nita, so he stayed with her, using his voice to soothe her and bring her back to herself.

After a few seemingly endless moments, Nita's glazed look transformed into her usual alertness. "I'm fine. What can I do? I don't know about the contractions. Want me to time them or something?"

"Yes. That would be perfect." That would give her something to focus on. "I'm going to work on getting a ride to the hospital. Tell Melissa I'll take care of it and not to panic. I'll make a couple of calls and be there in a second. And keep your cool, Nita. She needs you."

She nodded, her jaw clenched with determination, and ran off. Jeb called Brody first and filled him in. "Get on the first plane you can. Or drive. Call your OB/GYN and see what hospital we should head to."

"I'm on it."

Then he called 911 and explained the situation to the dispatcher, who was in Port Howard on the mainland. "I can send the fire boat, but it takes an hour to get out there. Maybe more in this weather."

"What about a Medevac?"

"They're all grounded at the moment due to lightning strikes. Might get the all clear soon, but I can't say when."

Jeb swore to himself, and hung up.

He called the Santa Lucia firehouse, but the phone did nothing but ring and ring. Maybe the line was out of order. Maybe everyone was out dealing with the storm. Maybe their incompetent fire chief was deep into a bottle of rum. He pulled out the pager Charlie had left him and punched in his cell number. A few seconds later Charlie called him back, sounding as if he was in the rinse cycle of a car wash.

Afraid the connection wouldn't last long, Jeb kept it simple. "We need to get Melissa to a hospital. Can you take us on your boat?"

Charlie's voice punched through the storm-static in

isolated words. ". . . fishing boat . . . cabin . . . uncomfortable . . ."

"Can you do it? Safely?"

". . . wharf . . . half an hour."

"We'll be there. Three of us." They would need Nita's help. He just hoped she was holding herself together enough to give it.

LIKE THE CARING friend she was, Nita came through. When he finally walked into Melissa's room, he found them sitting on the bed, Melissa holding onto Nita's hand for dear life while Nita stared at the timer on her iPhone.

"Her pains are lasting forty seconds," she said proudly. "And they're coming about eight minutes apart."

"*Eight* minutes?"

"Yes, is that bad?"

He recovered himself quickly. "No, that's fine. It looks like this baby likes to make things interesting."

Melissa's eyes brimmed with tears. "But Brody isn't here! I can't have the baby without Brody."

"He's on his way. He's going to meet us at the hospital."

Tears poured down Melissa's cheeks. "I should have listened to him. Why'd I have to go waltzing off to some island for a stupid story? Now the baby might be born without Brody, and I couldn't stand it if that happened."

"Shhh, shhh." Nita threw her arms around Melissa, who buried her head in Nita's shoulder. "It's going to be fine. Brody will get there. I mean, come on, he's Brody!

He'll find a way. And Jeb will get us to the hospital, right?"

"The boat's picking us up at the wharf in," he checked his watch, "twenty minutes. Nita, are you packed?"

Just then Melissa gave another deep groan and clutched at Nita. "I just need my purse," Nita told him. "Can you grab it?"

"Of course. Get Melissa to the Suburban and I'll be there in a few minutes." He picked up Melissa's bag and her laptop case. "Is this everything?"

"Yes," gasped Melissa, emerging from the contraction. "I travel light. Well, except for this belly I'm hauling around."

"Sense of humor. That's good. Hang onto that."

She did her best, he had to hand it to her. By the time they all made it to the wharf, they were drenched to the skin from the rain whipping through the air. It took all his driving skills to dodge the broken tree branches and tumbling lawn furniture clogging the roads. Both Melissa and Nita were great, keeping their cool through huge gusts of wind that shook the old Suburban.

At the wharf, Melissa's calm deserted her at the sight of Charlie's boat, which had an open deck, a tiny wheelhouse, and narrow benches as seats. "We're not going in that, are we?" she wailed. A breaking wave sent a plume of ocean water over them, making her stagger.

Jeb wiped salt water out of his eyes with one hand while the other held her steady. On Melissa's other side, Nita was shoving her drenched hair off her face.

"Are you sure about this, Jeb?" She called over the constant thunder of the surf.

"It's safe," he told them. "These boats are built to ride out storms."

Charlie called to them from the wheelhouse. "I know it looks bad, but this boat's been through worse storms than this. I can't leave the wheel while she's at the dock. Can you make it aboard okay?"

A large swell pushed the craft against the pilings, so hard the rubber fenders got squished to the side. For the first time, Jeb felt a moment of real fear. What if Melissa couldn't bridge the constantly shifting gap between the wharf and the boat? What if she *fell in*? Maybe they'd be safer staying on the island until the storm subsided. If the baby came, he could handle it. He was a trained EMT, and had handled many medical emergencies over the years.

But none of them had involved a late-term pregnant woman with premature rupture of the membranes. His expertise was just enough to know that she needed a damn doctor. They had to get on that boat.

"Is there a ramp we can use?" He called to Charlie. But just then, Jeb heard a shout and turned to see several other people in oilskins jogging down the wharf. Behind them he spotted the bright yellow Santa Lucia fire engine parked at the top of the long ramp. Relief flooded through him.

The Santa Lucia volunteer firefighters were coming to the rescue.

They cheerfully swarmed around Jeb, Melissa and

Nita. "Charlie got ahold of us," one of them explained. "We were clearing some downed power lines."

"You guys know the ocean better than I do," he told them. "How do we get her safely on that boat?"

"I'm right here," muttered Melissa.

Quickly, the firefighters organized themselves into a sort of bucket brigade, with two guys on the boat and two standing next to Melissa, each holding one of her arms. "When I say 'Go,' you step forward, ma'am," said one of them. "That's all you have to do. We'll do the rest. Sir, you can step back for a minute."

"You know what you're doing?"

"Boats, we know. It's the fires we're a little shaky on."

Muttering a quick prayer, Jeb stepped back. His hand slipped into Nita's. They clung to each other, holding their breath as they watched the firefighters poised for action. One of them made a smiling comment to Melissa, which seemed to relax her.

"They're good guys," Jeb murmured to Nita. "Really good guys."

And then, during the still moment between waves, when the ocean took a breath before its next onslaught, Melissa stepped forward. The two men onboard grabbed her by the arms as the other two let go. They leveraged her onto the deck of the boat, where she stood, shaking and laughing and bestowing kisses on each and every one of them.

"Come on," said Jeb. "Our turn." He propelled Nita forward, into the waiting arms of the firefighters.

They helped Nita aboard first, swinging her across the

spitting ocean in the same rhythm they'd used with Melissa. By then Jeb had gotten the hang of it and stepped onto the heaving deck by himself.

"You're a natural, sir," said one of the firemen. "Next time you come out we'll take you fishing."

"You're on." He clapped the nearest two on the back. "You guys keep up the good work."

"Will do, sir. You're in good hands with Charlie." They swarmed off the boat and waved goodbye as Charlie swung the wheel to guide them toward the tossing, rampaging ocean.

Away from the dock, the fishing boat's rocking, rolling motion felt like that of a bucking bronco. As soon as they hit the first swell, Melissa threw up. There was so much water running across the decks, rainwater and seawater mixed, that it got washed away in seconds.

"I can't go in that cabin," she gasped. "Too claustrophobic."

"That's fine. But you have to sit down." If she stood the whole time, she might slip and fall, or get knocked into the ocean.

He guided her to a spot where she could lean her back against the outer bulkhead of the cabin and helped her slide down until she sat, her legs stretched in front of her. Jeb crouched next to her, positioning his body so he was blocking some of the wind and sluicing water. Nita took the bags into the cabin, then came and settled next to Melissa. Nita put her arm around her friend, trying to keep her warm.

After a few more episodes of retching, Melissa closed

her eyes and seemed to slip into a trance. Maybe she found the slamming rhythm of the craft and the drone of the engine soothing. At any rate, unconsciousness seemed like an improvement.

"You can sleep too," he told Nita.

She looked at him as if he were nuts. "I can't sleep. I need to be here for her if she wakes up."

"I'm awake," Melissa murmured. "Just don't ask me anything challenging."

"Are you feeling okay?"

"I'm aiming for an out-of-body experience until I'm with Brody. Nothing counts until I see him."

Jeb exchanged a worried look with Nita. He didn't like the sound of "out-of-body experience."

"Anyway, you guys have plenty to talk about without me. You need to figure out how you're going to do this," Melissa said.

"An ambulance will be waiting for us at the ferry landing."

"Not that. You."

"Me?" Jeb pointed to himself in confusion.

"You and Nita."

Jeb's gaze flew to meet Nita's. It was hard to tell under all her wet, dark hair, but he thought she was blushing.

"What makes you think there's a Jeb and me?"

"Pregnant woman's intuition."

"Well, you're off base. It would never work out with me and Jeb." The boat crested a wave, the engine whining as it lost contact with the water. Then it slammed down, jarring every bone in Jeb's body.

The impact was nothing compared to that of Nita's statement. "Excuse me? Why not?"

"You just got out of a long marriage."

"I got divorced a year ago. And the 'marriage' part of the marriage died long before. Not a good reason."

"I'm still trying to get my life back on track after everything that happened."

"Okay, I'll give you that one. So we go slow. I'm not pushing anything on you."

"I'm not like Belinda."

"You're not gay? Glad to hear it."

"Okay, I'm officially asleep now," said Melissa. She faked a snore, then arched her back as another pain struck.

They helped her through it, letting her squeeze their hands until they turned white. When the pain had passed, and Melissa was once again discreetly pretending to sleep, Nita lowered her voice. "I can't do it, Jeb. Maybe you look at me and see someone who's very confident, but let me tell you, it's all a fake. That's how I became a press agent. Fake it till you make it; that was my motto. But you know what you can't fake? You can't fake making your boyfriend stick around. You can't fake making your *baby* stick around. That's the truth about me, Jeb. I'm a failure. Life has shredded me like . . . like . . . cabbage on a taco. *That's* why we can't get involved. That's why you should let it go. Before either of us . . . well, me . . . gets hurt."

"That's it? Your reason? Or is there more?" A slow fury was building inside him. She was ready to jettison not only him, but worse than that, herself.

"Th . . . that's it."

"If you think that's what I see when I look at you, you're dreaming. I don't see a failure or some kind of overconfident superwoman. I see a woman who I haven't been able to forget for three years—a woman who doesn't have to do anything but exist to make me want her. A woman who's so beautiful my eyes hurt from staring. A woman I want to talk to, and make love to, and sleep next to. You're not a failure. You're a beautiful, smart, compassionate woman who's taken some blows. Why does that mean you have to lock yourself in your little tower room and throw away the key?"

"I . . . I'm not throwing anything away."

"You're throwing us away."

"But—"

"Take a look around you. We're on a little fishing boat in the middle of an ocean that's trying to drown us, in a rainstorm trying to do the same, with a woman who could give birth at any moment. Do you think this is safe?"

Melissa piped up with a sound of alarm, but Jeb barreled right over her. "No, it's not safe. It's *life*."

Chapter Eleven

AS IF EMPHASIZING Jeb's point, a curling wave swept across the deck, splashing a huge amount of shockingly cold water in Nita's face. She squeezed her eyes shut and hunched her body against the force of it. When she opened them again, she saw Jeb braced protectively over Melissa. His back was completely drenched. Melissa shivered violently.

"Everyone okay back there?" Charlie called.

"Nita, can you crawl into the wheelhouse and ask if he has any extra gear we can use?"

Nita did as he suggested, making her way on hands and knees into the little wheelhouse. Standing up seemed much too risky. She came back with an extra rain jacket made from thick orange rubbery material. Jeb draped it over Melissa, and they spent the rest of the wild trip huddled together in the corner of the fishing boat. No more talking. That was fine with Nita; Jeb had already given her enough to think about.

When they reached the wharf, the boat riding up against the pilings, Melissa finally opened her eyes. Even though the harbor was much calmer than the wild open ocean, the waves still tossed them around like a bath toy.

"We made it," Melissa gasped, as Nita and Jeb helped her to her feet. "Where's Brody?"

"He'll be here soon," Nita told her, hoping to God it was true.

Melissa let out a wrenching sob. "I need him. I need Brody." The words were like a primal cry ripped from her heart. Nita felt tears run down her own face.

Jeb steered Melissa toward the gunwales of the boat. His brisk tone acted like a tonic. "No losing it now, Melissa. Brody's meeting us at the hospital. We have to get you off this boat so we can find him. Now say goodbye to Charlie."

Charlie finished fastening the lines to cleats on the wharf, and hurried to join them. "Sorry it was a bit rough out there. On Santa Lucia we say it's good luck to be born during a storm."

Melissa's face, drenched with tears and ocean spray, brightened. "We'll name the baby Hurricane or something. Stormcloud."

"Seasick's a pretty word, if you don't think about the meaning," Nita threw in. Melissa laughed, which Nita considered a personal triumph. Jeb shot her a grateful smile, which made her feel like a million bucks.

An ambulance, lights flashing, swung into view. Two paramedics jumped out and dashed toward them. Jeb waved them over, and gave them a quick rundown in medical jargon while Nita supported Melissa.

Then they were whisking her off. Nita's last glimpse of Melissa was of her white face and brave wave. "See you at the hospital," she called to her. "We'll be right behind you."

Charlie shoved aside his oilskins and dug in his pocket. "Take my car," he told them. "It's the old yellow mustang parked around the corner."

"Charlie," Jeb began, then broke off as a powerful emotion gripped him. He swallowed, cleared his throat, then tried again. "You did good. Real good."

"Yeah?" The kid's face lit up. "Even compared to a real fireman?"

"You are real. Real as anyone. If you ever need anything, you call me. If you come to San Gabriel, first round's on me. And the second. In fact, don't even bother to bring your wallet."

Charlie grinned. "Who are you kidding? You won't be able to stay away from San-L. You can buy me a shot at Old Mort's. I gotta get back out and see what kind of mess the guys are dealing with. Leave my car keys with the harbormaster if you aren't coming back."

With a last wave, he jumped back on his boat. Nita watched him go, blinking away her own tears. That cheerful young sprig of a man had saved them. But Jeb had made it possible. Without Jeb . . . she shuddered. She didn't even want to think about that.

"Come on," he said now, grabbing her hand. "I don't know when Brody's going to get here, and Melissa needs familiar faces. You ready?"

She nodded. Maybe she ought to feel awkward, since she didn't really know where they stood, she and Jeb, after that conversation on the boat. But she didn't feel awkward. The only thing she felt was gratitude for his quick-thinking, rock-solid presence, and pure happiness to be holding his hand.

He didn't let go much at all during the drive to the County Hospital. Only when he had to shift gears or make an extreme turn. They stayed latched together, unwilling to lose contact, as they located the hospital, parked, and made their way into the emergency room. The charge nurse directed them to the maternity ward.

"That means it's really happening," Jeb murmured. "The baby's coming. Brody better get here soon."

AN HOUR LATER, Brody burst into the waiting room of the maternity ward, waking Nita from her exhausted slumber against Jeb's shoulder. Anchored by Jeb's arm, surrounded by the scent of his leather jacket and the ocean salt drying on his body, she'd slipped into a delicious sleep. But the wild-eyed man who careened into the hospital lounge changed all that.

"Stone!" He practically leaped across the room. His hair stood up from his head in all directions. Nita had always known Brody as a powerfully contained, calm sort of man. She'd never seen this side of him. "Where is she? How's she doing? What did the doctor say?"

"She's fine. Premature membrane rupture, she's been in labor for about two hours. They said you should go in as soon as you get here. She's been asking for you every two minutes."

"Thank God. I'm going." He turned, then spun back around and yanked Jeb into a hard hug. "I owe you, man."

"No you don't. What are brothers for?"

"I'll never forget this."

Then it was Nita's turn. Brody hugged her too, then speared her with that intense charcoal-gray gaze. Suddenly she felt like a bedraggled duckling with her damp hair hanging down her back. "Thanks for taking care of my heart," he said seriously. Then he was gone, leaving Nita to sink back into the chair next to Jeb and ponder his phrasing.

His heart. Melissa was his heart, his core. He must have been terrified of losing her. Melissa must feel something similar every time she watched Brody head to the fire station. Storms, fires, accidents . . . anything could happen. But that didn't keep Brody and Melissa from loving each other with all their hearts.

Jeb was right. Avoiding love might keep her safe. But was that the life she wanted?

She stole a sidelong glance at him. His legs were stretched to their full length, his head tilted back. His eyes were closed, those thick black eyelashes vulnerable against his cheeks. Soft snores riffled his nostrils. He'd worked so hard to get them here, to stand in for Brody, to keep Melissa safe and her spirits high. No wonder he was exhausted.

She curled up against him, even though the armrest between their two seats dug into her ribs. Her desire to be close to him kept growing with every second she spent with him. The shocking truth was . . . the shocking truth was . . . she'd fallen for him.

Maybe he didn't want what she wanted. Maybe it was too soon for him to be in a relationship. But that was her overactive brain talking. Ask her heart, and none of that mattered. She'd fallen for him, and she'd have to take her chances.

As soon as they both woke up.

BUT WHEN SHE finally opened her eyes, there was a new baby boy to meet. She and Jeb, holding hands, stepped into the room where Melissa lay with a tiny bundle nestled on her shoulder. Brody had practically climbed into the hospital bed with her, and seemed completely unable to tear his eyes off his brand new son.

Melissa looked surprisingly chipper. "I'm going to recommend to all my friends that they take a boat ride through a storm right before they have their babies. It was such a relief not to be rocking around anymore, labor was almost a piece of cake. Almost," she emphasized. She'd always been a very accurate reporter.

Nita drew close, marveling at the tiny creature's deep, trusting sleep and miniature body parts. "Wow. Just look at him. He's perfect."

"He's tough. Chip off the block, no doubt. He came a month early for no particular reason, and everything's fine. No problems at all." Her eyes swam with sudden tears. "Darn, I thought once the baby came I'd stop getting so emotional. No such luck. Sorry, Brody."

"That's all right. I think it's catching." Seemingly hypnotized, Brody lifted the tiny boy's little finger with his own large one. The sight made Nita's heart clench. This was one lucky baby, to have a father like Brody. She glanced at Jeb, and drew in a breath. His usually hard face had relaxed, his tiger eyes held a quiet, happy glow. And she realized that, in at least one respect, she was completely wrong about him. This man wouldn't object to more children. Family was everything to him. Even when his wife discovered her attraction to women and divorced him, he still considered her family.

Suddenly tears began spilling down her cheeks in unstoppable streams. She swiped at them, caught Melissa's concerned look, tried to speak, couldn't. Finally she gasped, "Be right back," and dashed for the hallway. She stumbled to the ladies' room, shut herself in a stall, buried her head in her hands, and surrendered to the wrenching sobs.

The tears had finally caught up with her. She'd stayed one step ahead of them—using work, the senator's crisis, Angie's need for help, anything that came along. They'd dogged her all the way to Santa Lucia Island and back, through a media storm and a real one, until they cornered her in a county hospital bathroom.

So . . . fine.

She cried, and cried. She let the tears wash away her grief, her sadness. Let them honor her loss. Let them bear witness to her pain. Let them drown her need to succeed under a waterfall of emotion. Losing a baby didn't make her a failure. Losing Bradford didn't make her a failure.

She'd never be perfect . . . and yet she was already perfect. Perfect as that little baby boy in there. Perfect as the baby who was never born. Perfect as the exhaustion on Melissa's face, the love in Brody's eyes. Perfect as the care of all the strangers who helped bring their child safely into the world.

Wounds and flaws didn't make her less perfect. They made her more perfectly human.

When she finally emerged from the bathroom, eyes still puffy from tears, Jeb was waiting for her.

"Better?" he asked, after a long, thoughtful moment of scrutiny.

She nodded. And it was true. She did feel a bit better. Maybe it was thanks to the release of that storm of tears. Maybe helping Melissa bring her baby safely into the world had helped heal some of her own pain. Or maybe . . . slowly, softly, she raised a hand to Jeb's cheek, and watched his eyes darken . . . maybe it was thanks to the magical presence of Jeb Stone. Blunt, honest Jeb, who knew how to face things head on.

Realizing she was staring at him with, very likely, an embarrassing amount of adoration, she tried to pull her gaze away. Then she stopped. No sense in hiding her feelings. And looking at him felt so good—like something she could do for a very long time.

He held her gaze without hesitation, which made her heart melt even more. Jeb would never back away, never leave her hanging. It wasn't in his nature. A smile spread across her face. It felt like the sun breaking through after a long rainy season.

Jeb turned his head sideways to press a kiss into her palm. "I had a thought," he told her in a gruff voice.

"What's that?"

"I was thinking that, after the dust settles and we get Melissa and Brody and the little guy squared away, we could continue our date."

"Continue our date?" For a moment, she had no idea what he was talking about. The time when she didn't know Jeb Stone seemed like a million years ago.

"Sure. And I know exactly where we can go."

Chapter Twelve

Pacific Ocean—Two months later

SANTA LUCIA ISLAND spread across the horizon like an enormous sage-green whale. Jeb sheltered Nita within the circle of his arms as they leaned on the railing of the *Danny B*. The scent of her hair, sweet as orange blossoms, mingled with the brisk saltiness of the ocean breeze. The flat Pacific sported an innocent air, as if to say, *Who me? I had nothing to do with that crazy storm. Don't blame me.*

Jeb dropped a kiss on the top of Nita's head. He could do that sort of thing now. Over the past two months they'd talked on the phone every day, often several times a day. He'd followed her job-hunting process, which she was conducting in a desultory manner that gave him some hope. If she wanted to stay in Los Angeles, he could live with that. He'd have to put in a transfer request, and probably drop back a level, but he'd made his peace with that possibility.

On the other hand, she'd visited him several times in San Gabriel, and loved it. But there wasn't much demand for press secretaries in a little town like that. He recognized that she needed something to pour her energy and skills into. She could run the whole town, as far as he was concerned, though she didn't seem inclined to stay in politics. But he'd be thrilled if she came to live in San Gabriel, as long as that's what she wanted. So would Alison, who seemed to look at their relationship as her personal achievement. The words "prayer flag" and "chant" had come up a bit too much for Jeb's comfort.

In his opinion, this miraculous new relationship had nothing to do with supernatural forces. It belonged to him and Nita. Well, maybe Melissa had something to do with it, since he'd followed her to Santa Lucia. And Brody, since he'd asked Jeb to follow her. Hell, maybe even Senator Stryker ought to be thanked for causing a scandal.

For sure, Melissa and Brody's little boy, named Lucius, had been essential. He and Nita, as godparents, would never forget it.

Charlie, practically bouncing with excitement, met them at the wharf. "Guess what just happened. Seriously, guess."

"Senator Stryker's running for president," suggested Nita.

"What?" He did a double take. "No. The fire chief quit! Well, he went into rehab and then wrote on his Facebook page that San-L has too many triggers and he's not coming back."

"Good," said Jeb, shouldering his bag and following Charlie up the ramp. "You guys deserve a good chief."

"We sure do." He sent Jeb a significant look, then when he got no response, tried it again.

Jeb gave him a severe frown. "No."

"All we ask is that you think—"

"No."

"But why—"

"I'm on a date. I don't like to think about work when I'm on a date."

"But we're desperate." Charlie opened the Enchanted Garden's Suburban and heaved their bags in the back. "The town council put an ad in the Help Wanted section and we've got nothing but wackos applying. Even Old Mort said he'd do it in a pinch."

"They're desperate," Nita teased Jeb after they'd all settled into their seats. "They're desperately seeking a fire chief. How can you resist?"

"I can't resist anything Nita says," Jeb told Charlie. "Maybe I'll come by the station later."

The kid let out a wolf howl of delight. As they rattled up the road that led to the Enchanted Garden, he added, "When I heard you were coming, I thought it was for the job."

"No. Melissa and her husband gave us this trip," explained Nita. "They wanted us to come back to the island where it all began."

"Interesting," mused Charlie. "Very interesting."

"What do you mean?"

"You'll see. I'm not saying anything else. Just that I bet Melissa's been talking to a certain someone around here."

Jeb and Nita shared a mystified glance. Charlie snapped his mouth shut and refused to say another word until they reached the Enchanted Garden. And then the sign posted on the lawn spoke for him. It could barely be read through the profusion of dahlias, a neon mélange of orange and yellow. But there it was: *For Sale by Owner.*

Nita's eyes went wide as the flowers. "Angie's *selling* the place?" She burst out of the van and ran to the front lawn. Angie emerged from the front door with a big soup pot. Just as she was about to ladle vegetable soup onto the marigolds, Nita stopped her with a gentle touch and said something Jeb couldn't hear.

He grabbed their bags, waved goodbye to Charlie, and joined Angie and Nita. Angie didn't seem to remember them. "Are you here about the ad I put in the paper? 'Enchanted Garden Seeks Queen of the Flowers'?"

"I didn't see it, but I have a feeling my friend did," Nita told her. "I'm very interested, though. We're staying for a few days, so we can talk more about it."

So Nita was "very interested," was she? Was she interested in knowing what he thought about it?

For that matter, what did he think about it?

"Oh, lovely!" Angie exclaimed. "It's so nice to have guests. You know, Clint Eastwood stayed here recently."

"Is that right?"

"Well, it might be or it might not be. Who knows?" She smiled cheerfully and trundled back inside. Jeb noticed that a crochet hook dangled from the back of her sweater, bouncing with each step.

LATER, IN THE turret room, Jeb spread Nita out as if the bed was a picnic blanket and she the feast. He let his tongue roam at will, starting with the inner swell of her calves, and heading toward heaven. He nibbled his way up her golden thighs, alternating little nips with long, soothing strokes that made her groan. From the way her hips rose to meet him, he knew he was driving her crazy. But not crazy enough.

He swerved around the downy mound that made his mouth water. As much as he wanted to devour her sweet sex, first he wanted to finish what he'd started. He had nipples to play with, erect little nubs that sent him mad with desire. Plump breasts cried out to be tasted. Each delicious curve demanded its due, from tongue or teeth, or the caress of his hand. He felt the dew rise on her skin, heard her breathing turn to a shudder.

"You taste like roses," he murmured. Unable to resist any longer, he put his mouth on her wet center. She arched upward, bunching the sheets in her fists.

"Maybe I'm the Queen of the Flowers," she gasped.

"Quite likely," he mumbled, her honey running over his tongue. She cried out, twisting as ecstasy seized her in its grip. He was so hard it hurt, but nothing gave him greater pleasure than milking every last spasm of pleasure from his woman.

His woman.

So maybe, just maybe, Belinda had taken a toll on his manhood. If so, he'd gotten it back with Nita—a hundred-fold. Nita liked it when he got wild. She liked it when he flipped her over, yanked her ass up in the air, spread her open and sheathed himself in her heat. Quite possibly she loved it, given how her inner walls sucked at his erection, given how she shifted her ass to take him deeper. He knew she loved it. He knew he loved *her*. With that thought, he exploded into her trembling body, his orgasm hitting him hard and fast, ripping a groan from his throat.

She was sobbing out her own orgasm. He felt the ripples up and down his cock. *God.* Could anything be better than this?

Yes, he thought, as they lay belly-to-belly, clasped tight in each other's arms. Knowing they could do this every night of their lives, and during the day as well, would be better.

"Let's buy the place," he said. "Let's buy it and start serving actual coffee and maybe even eggs and bacon in the mornings. And cut the ruffle count in half."

"What?" She mumbled, already starting to drift off.

"I'll check into the fire chief job. If that doesn't work out, I can volunteer. In my spare time I can fix faucets. You can run the bed and breakfast."

"You have it all planned out, do you?" Wide awake now, she tilted her head back on the pillow, her sweat-dampened hair sticking to her neck. Tenderly he freed the strands and smoothed them out behind her.

"I'm organized that way. Admit it, you've been think-ing about it too."

"Well, sure, I admit it. I've barely been thinking about anything else except for your hot, steamy sexiness."

He smiled. His woman sure had a way with words.

"But I didn't know how you felt," she continued.

"That part's simple enough. I want to be with you. I love you." The words slipped out without deliberate thought. At her soft indrawn breath, he realized that he'd never actually said them before. He'd thought it often enough. But maybe the words hadn't made their way to the surface. "I know it's still, maybe, a little early, though they say that extreme circumstances speed things up, and I know that you're possibly still—"

"No, I'm not. It's not. It's perfect. I love you too. I love you so much." Her earnest gaze clung to his. "But I have to know something. How do you feel about having children? Maybe you don't want any more? Or maybe you do, and you'll be disappointed if I can't conceive?"

"Honey." He cupped her face in his hand. "I want *you*. We'll figure the rest out. You know me. I'm a travel-the-road-you're-on kind of guy. Whatever comes, we'll make it work. And we'll have fun making it work. That part I'm sure about."

She stared at him, her expression inscrutable in the cool moonlight. Was she chewing on the inside of her cheek again? Had he made her anxious?

He didn't want to cause her stress. All he wanted was to love her and support her while she threw herself into whatever endeavor she chose. "Is that a good enough answer?" he asked.

"Oh yeah," she sighed. "It's perfect."

Want more sexy firemen?
Keep reading for a sneak peek at Vader's story in

FOUR WEDDINGS AND A FIREMAN,

coming in March 2014
from Avon Books!

An Excerpt from

FOUR WEDDINGS AND A FIREMAN

Prologue

At the wedding of Sabina Jones and
Chief Rick Roman . . .

DEREK "VADER" BROWN could bench-press nearly twice his own weight and heave an unconscious fire victim of any shape or size over one shoulder, but weddings turned him into a ball of mush. When a bride walked down the aisle, he might as well be some mutant combination of a puppy dog and a marshmallow, especially when that bride was his best friend, Sabina Jones, joining in true love and matrimony with Chief Roman.

If only Sabina hadn't begged Vader to be her "man of honor." If only he hadn't invited Cherie Harper, the girl he'd been seeing on and off for a year, the girl he couldn't stop thinking about even during those "off" times. If only he hadn't happened to glance her way while the preacher discussed good times and bad.

But he did, and the dreamy smile on Cherie's face was the nail in the coffin of his dignity.

Blame it on the orange blossom high. Blame it on the look of rapture on Sabina's face as Roman claimed his first married kiss. Whatever the reason, soon after the "I do's" had been said, Vader found himself circling the dance floor with Cherie in his arms, blurting words he hadn't consciously decided to utter.

"Marry me."

Cherie stumbled. Not a good sign, since she taught dance. Her gray eyes flew to meet his, and all he read in them was wariness. "What did you say?"

Slightly shocked, Vader replayed the words in his mind and decided that he stood by them. Despite their ups and downs, he loved Cherie passionately. He knew she loved him too, even though she fought against it.

"Marry me. Be my bride." His heart swelled. This was right. It felt right. Saying those words aloud made all his confused emotions about Cherie settle into place, like puzzle pieces fitting together. Cherie was the right woman for him, the only woman for him. "I promise I'll take care of you and make you happy, all that good stuff."

But Cherie seemed to be going through an entirely different set of emotions, judging by the anguish on her face. "Honey, you know how I feel about you. But I can't marry you," she whispered gently.

Vader's world went still, as if a bubble had dropped around the two of them. Outside the bubble, everyone else grooved to the tune of "Love Will Keep Us Together."

Inside, things were a lot more confusing. "Why not? I'd be a great husband."

"You'd be the best husband in the world." Tears welled in her eyes, turning them silver. "But I'm not interested in getting married to anyone. Please just believe me, Vader, please?"

She seemed so upset, he swallowed back his protest. He looked away, only to encounter one blissful couple after another. Captain Brody and Melissa glowed with the joy of brand-new parents. Ryan Blake and his wife, Katie, were cracking up as they tried out some complicated new dance step. Thor and Maribel, who had flown down from Alaska for the wedding, beamed with their own good news—pregnant with twins. Captain Jeb Stone was whispering something to his brand new fiancée, Nita Moreno. Everywhere Vader looked, happy faces stared back.

Except for the one in front of him. Cherie had gone pale with distress. "Can we just erase the last two minutes?" she asked in a pleading tone. "Go back to how things were?"

Erase his proposal? He wrestled with that one for a long minute. Granted, he hadn't exactly meant to propose. It was a spur-of-the-moment thing, and obviously a huge mistake. Why did the thought of marriage get her so upset? Didn't most people want to get married?

He squinted at her, slightly dizzy from spinning across the dance floor under the influence of many champagne toasts. He hated upsetting Cherie. He'd jumped the gun and fucked this up. He had only himself to blame.

Even though it hurt his heart, he forced himself to nod. "Forget it. Weddings always mess me up. Now what were we talking about? Grey's Anatomy, right?"

Her face lit up and she threw her arms around him. The feel of her curvy body, so warm and womanly, took some of the sting out of the moment.

He gathered her close and rested his cheek on her soft hair, which was currently blond with pink stripes. He inhaled a deep breath of lilac-scented essence of Cherie. They'd survive this. He didn't give up that easy. At the right moment, he'd try again. In the meantime, he'd stay away from weddings.

Four months and twelve days later, at the wedding of Patrick Callahan IV and Lara Nelson . . .

THE RING OF her phone startled Cherie awake. Disoriented, she scrambled for it, squinting at the name that flashed on the screen. Vader. What in blue blazes? Vader was in Loveless, Nevada at the wedding of his friend Patrick. And it was three in the morning.

Oh, sweet Lord. A wedding. She'd nearly forgotten what happened at the last one. The smart thing would be to ignore the call in case Vader did anything reckless like throw their relationship into chaos again.

Still, it was Vader, her own personal version of catnip, the only substance in the world she couldn't resist for long. "Hello?"

Vader's deep voice rumbled from her phone, sending

the usual shivers down her spine. "We should get married, Cherie."

Crap.

"I mean it," he continued. "Why don't you fly down here right away and I'll pick you up in Psycho's tractor and we'll get ourselves hicced. I mean, hitched."

"Vader, are you drunk?" Was Vader drunk-dial proposing to her? Despite her sinking heart, a little snort of laughter escaped her.

"Oh come on, Cherie. You know we're meant to be together. You know it. Hang on. Some dude's banging on the door."

"Where are you?"

"Bathroom."

"You're proposing to me in a bathroom?"

"Dude! Find yourself a bush. Toilet's taken." He returned to her. "Some guys have no manners. Frickin' embarrassment."

Cherie clapped a hand over her mouth to keep from giggling out loud. "Let's talk later, okay?"

"I can't stay in here all night. People won't like that."

"No, I mean, let's talk tomorrow. When the wedding's totally over and you've had a good night's sleep."

Vader went quiet. Then, "Aw, hell."

"What?"

"I proposed again, didn't I? And you rejected me."

"Vader. I didn't reject you because you didn't propose. You're a little buzzed, and I'm half asleep, and none of this counts." Please, just let him forget the whole thing ever happened.

"You wanna erath . . . erase it, don't you? Just like last time?"

Cherie groaned silently. "Could we?"

"Guys don't like having their proposals erased. Feels bad."

No, no, no. Cherie hated hurting anyone, but hurting Vader was the worst of all. She couldn't bear it. "Please don't feel bad, sweetheart. You know how I feel about you. This is just bad timing, that's all. We'll talk about it later." She cast around for a distraction. "How was the wedding?"

"Beautiful. That's the problem, right there. Weddings. I can't take it. They're too freaking beautiful. The way Lara looked at Psycho, like he's made out of stardust or something . . . and the llama . . . the cute little llama had the ring tied to her collar and she trotted up right when she was supposed to, and—" He broke off.

"Vader? Are you okay?"

"I better go."

"Are we cool? Still friends?"

Vader let out a long groan. "We are what we are, tha's all. Whatever that is. And don' ask me to figure it out. I'm done trying, Cherie. Done." And the connection ended.

Cherie dropped back on her pillow, then grabbed another one and clamped it over her mouth so she could let out a frustrated scream. If only she could explain everything to Vader . . . but she couldn't.

This was a disaster. Vader had now proposed twice. In the morning, he'd probably hate her. What if he hated her so much he decided to call it quits, for real? The thought gave her a horrible chill. Life without Vader . . . she didn't want to think about it. Vader was too important to her.

They'd survive this. She didn't give up that easily. At the right moment, she'd try to get their relationship back on track.

With her natural optimism flowing back, she searched for a bright side and finally found one.

Vader was one of the famous Bachelor Firemen of San Gabriel. Bachelor Firemen. As in, single. Surely that meant no more weddings for a while. If the Bachelor Firemen would just stop getting married, Vader would forget about proposing and they could go back to normal. She floated a tiny prayer into the heavens. Let the Bachelor Firemen curse last just a little bit longer.

Chapter One

VADER, WEARING FIREFIGHTER'S pants, suspenders, and nothing else, bent the giggling blond girl backward over his left arm, flexed his right biceps, and grinned for the camera. "How does that look?"

Stupid, mouthed Fred, also known as Stud, who was manning the Firefighter Photo Booth.

"Perfect," squealed the girl. "It looks like you're saving me from a fire, right?"

"Well, I normally wouldn't fight a fire without my shirt on." He lowered his voice to Elvis Presley-range and wiggled his eyebrows. "Except on certain special occasions."

She laughed and playfully swatted his chest, letting her hand linger. Vader plastered the grin back on his face, added a little Elvis lip curl, and jerked his head for Fred to take the photo. As soon as the telltale click had sounded, he dropped the pose and planted the girl back on her feet.

"Whew," she said, a little breathless at the speed with which she'd been righted. "You sure are strong. Do you work out?"

Vader caught a spluttering sound from Fred's direction.

"In our job, it pays to be fit," Vader told the girl. Her gaze drifted back and forth over the musculature of his torso. He fought the urge to say, 'Eyes up here.' "The better to rescue pretty girls from all those fiery infernos."

She sighed at the prospect of a fiery inferno. But Vader wasn't paying attention to her anymore; Cherie was somewhere in the crowd. He knew it, even though he couldn't exactly say how. Maybe he'd caught a glimpse of her hair, currently the color of Hot Tamales, through the throng of visitors. Maybe he'd heard a thread of her voice, that silvery, tender, maddening voice of hers, between the shouts of the Muster Games participants scrambling to don turnouts. Or maybe it was his sixth sense that always responded whenever Cherie was near.

Stud brought the photo to the blond girl, who by now had realized that Vader's gaze had wandered. She shifted her attention to Fred.

"Hey, you're kinda cute too," she told Stud. "Are you a Bachelor Fireman?"

"We don't really call ourselves that." Fred reddened. According to local legend, a volunteer fireman from the 1850s, thwarted in love when his mail-order bride ran off with a robber, laid a curse on the station. Since, in the time-honored tradition of firemen everywhere, his fellow firefighters had relentlessly teased him about his broken

heart, he'd vowed that every San Gabriel fireman forever-
more should suffer in love the way he had.

The curse certainly seemed to apply to Vader and
Fred, both of whom were still single.

"You want a picture with Stud too? I'll take it," offered
Vader. Normally he liked feminine attention. In fact, he
loved it. But this thing with Cherie had been knocking
him off his game for a while. Two failed proposals took it
out of a guy. He'd been avoiding her since Psycho's wedding two weeks ago. He wasn't sure what she was doing
here. Hope for Firefighters was his turf.

He realized the girl was waving a hand in front of his
face. "You all right there, big guy?"

"Sure. Little thirsty. Hot day, huh? Hey, you have fun
today. Thanks for supporting the San Gabriel Fire Department, we sure do appreciate it." He moved her away
from the backdrop under the guise of reaching for a water
bottle. With a sulky pout, she snatched up her photo and
wandered to the next booth, where Ace, the blond surfer-
boy rookie, was serving up his mother's Southern fried
chicken.

"I need a bathroom break," said Fred, slapping a
"Closed" sign on the photo booth. "Be right back." He
hurried away as Vader slouched against one of the saw-
horses that partitioned off their area. Three city blocks
had been cleared of cars for the Hope for Firefighters
event. White canopied stands lined both sides of the
street, and happy crowds of sweaty San Gabriel residents
strolled from one to the next. Vader loved this event, because he actually got to talk to people when they were in

a good mood, rather than terrified, traumatized, or unconscious.

He tilted his head back and let the water flow into his mouth. It was a scorching hot August day. The force of the sun overhead was nearly physical, reminding him of the way air heated by a fire beat against his body. A few stray drops of water rolled down his throat and chest, offering some welcome relief. He should have signed up for the dunk tank. But since he, more than anyone else at the station, fit the image of a macho, ridiculously muscled superhero-type, once again he'd been given photo booth duty.

Last year. He swore it. He was becoming a cliché.

"Isn't that your friend, Cherie?" A smirky male voice caught his attention. "I think he's trying out for a Crystal Geyser ad. Hand me the camera, Nick."

Vader groaned. He knew that voice. While he didn't hate anyone—it wasn't in his nature—if he'd hated someone, it would be the owner of that voice, Soren. He was one of Cherie's housemates, the other being Nick. Soren and Nick had an emo-goth-trance band called Optimal Doom, which for some reason they thought was super-hip.

Vader refused to say what he thought. Cherie's housemates were friends of her brother Jacob, and she was fiercely, unshakably loyal to her brother.

Reluctantly, he turned his head. And there she was, standing just behind the two weedy guys in their black T-shirts, her cinnamon-red hair in a haphazard pile, a little sundress the color of pink lemonade skimming her generous curves, looking so delicious every muscle in his body clenched.

She smiled uncertainly at him and gave a little wave. He frowned at her. How dare she smile at him, after shooting him down a second time?

She lifted her chin and intensified her smile. That was Cherie. Always determined to make the best of things and stay friends, no matter what. "Yes, that's my buddy Vader."

Buddy? Buddy? Vader saw red. She didn't call him her "buddy" when she screamed his name in mid-orgasm, she didn't call him "buddy" when he tied her to the bedposts—granted, she'd been pissed that he'd used his socks, but that hadn't stopped her from coming three times and . . .

He shook himself to attention just as Soren took a picture of him, most likely looking like an idiot as he gaped at them over an empty water bottle. "That'll be five dollars for the photo," he told Soren.

"But I didn't pose with you."

"Doesn't matter. If you want a picture of me, it's five dollars."

"Dude, get real. This is a public place. I can take whatever pictures I want."

Vader's jaw tightened. "This is a charity event. It's five dollars."

"Then I take my picture back. Here." He deleted the photo from his camera. "Gone." He smirked. "No more Poland Springs ad for you."

"Hey," Cherie protested. "Was that necessary?"

Vader would have liked to pick the loser up and launch him toward the dunk tank, but he reminded himself that Cherie appreciated Soren's prompt rent payments. "Let me guess. You guys have been walking around here, taking pictures and making fun of stuff, and you haven't bought one thing yet."

The two guys looked at each other, smirking. "Yeah, pretty much."

He shook his head, disgusted, and turned away. They weren't worth his time. He didn't know why Cherie put up with them. Maybe it was just one more indication of how wrong for each other he and Cherie were.

Too bad the rest of him didn't seem to believe that. Even now, a little current of electricity was racing through his body.

"Don't you worry, I'm spending enough money for all of us," said Cherie, with a trace of a Southern accent and another determined smile. "I got a Sloppy Joe from Ryan that was pretty much out of this world. I bought a whole strip of those raffle tickets. They said the prize was a Firefighter for a Day." She gave a nervous little laugh. "No wonder they're going so fast."

Cherie was always innocently making comments that others could interpret as lascivious, as he was doing at this very moment. Then she'd realize it, and two spots of pink would appear on her cheeks and . . .

Vader didn't want to look back at her, fought not to do so. He fixed his gaze on the orange and black swirls of the photo backdrop, but damn it, when it came to Cherie, his willpower evaporated faster than mist in the July heat. He gave in and let his eyes travel back to her. She was digging in her little silver purse, the one that was shaped like a dog bone. She triumphantly held up a twenty-dollar bill.

"And now I'd like a photo with San Gabriel's sexiest fireman."

"You're going to pay twenty bucks for a picture of you and your ex?" Soren laughed.

Nick chimed in. "Maybe he'll make his pecs do a little jig for the camera."

Vader clenched his hands into fists so tight, they could have broken through steel. Sure, he played the clown sometimes. He liked to bring a smile to people's faces. That didn't give them the right to—

A soft hand on his forearm interrupted his train of thought. "Ignore them," Cherie whispered. The scent of lilac, her favorite, surrounded him, making him feel as if he'd just lain down in a spring meadow with Cherie beside him. "They're just being jerks. Because they can. Now come on, let me make it up to you. Twenty dollars for a photo."

He pulled his arm away from her touch. "I don't think so, Cherie."

"Why not, for mercy's sake? It's for charity. Think of all those widows and orphans."

He pulled her aside, well out of earshot of her house-mates. "Why did you come here?"

Her lips parted, as if he'd taken her off guard. They were distractingly curvy, just like the rest of her. She studied him with serious gray eyes. They weren't really gray, he knew. One afternoon, during a picnic, he'd spent a long time studying them, noticing concentric rings and identifying their colors. The shimmery green of dew-covered grass, the deep gold of an antique picture frame, the gray of evening fog over a lake. "Vader, please. I support the fire department just like everyone else here. I support you. And I wanted to see you. I . . . I missed you. Vader, you're . . . well, you're very dear to me. You know you are."

He groaned out loud. No freaking willpower. "You turned me down, Cherie. Twice."

"I thought we were going to erase all that. Besides, I wouldn't put it like that. What I said was that I wasn't interested in getting married. Lots of people aren't."

"Yes, but your eyelid twitched."

"Excuse me?"

"Don't you know that your right eyelid twitches when you're not telling the whole truth? I've really got to get you to a poker table one of these days."

Her hand flew to her right eye. "It does not."

"Fine. Five-card stud, dollar a point."

Just then Fred came back and flipped the sign back to "Open."

"Hey, Cherie." He glanced at Vader, clearly looking for a clue as to how friendly he should be to her. Vader shrugged, and Fred's smile broadened. "Great to see you. Ready for your close-up?"

"You know it. Now, Stud, I'm paying extra for this baby, so make it good."

He handed her a helmet. "Why don't you put that on? It'd be cute."

Vader knew plenty of girls who wouldn't have wanted to mess up their hair with a clunky, heavy old fireman's helmet. But Cherie was game for anything. She grinned at Fred, then gave Vader the helmet. "Hold it for a sec, please."

She reached into her pile of hair and pulled out the pins that were holding everything in place up there. A torrent of spicy, sun-spangled hair came tumbling down over her bare shoulders.

Vader ground his teeth against the inevitable hardening of his body. Did she have to be so damn sexy? She planted the helmet on her head, and he lifted his eyes to the heavens, wondering just what he'd done to make the Almighty torture him like this. She looked . . . adorable. And he adored her. That's all there was to it.

And that's all there'd ever be. Him, adoring her. Her, back and forth about him.

He took a deep breath and stepped toward her. He could suffer a little more, for charity. Widows and orphans. Widows and orphans. "Come on. Let's get in front of the backdrop."

Cherie glanced at the sheet of plywood behind them. It featured dramatic flames and billowing smoke taken from a close-up of an apartment fire. "The photo's going to show a fire raging behind us?"

Hopefully it wouldn't also show the fire raging inside him. He wondered if she felt a fraction of the lust scorching through his veins.

Soren hooted with laughter. "That's called the fire down below, babe."

She shot her housemate a scathing look. "Shut up, Soren. You're acting like an idiot."

Instantly, the guy piped down. Vader rolled his eyes. Cherie loved to mother people, and in the case of her housemates, that included trying to correct their rude manners. Maybe he should let her boss him around too. But, no. He had too much leader-of-the-pack, take-charge, tough-guy in him. He'd tried to tone it down, but what was the point? He'd never be the emo type. He'd never be Nick.

Which gave him an idea. In one swift motion, he swept Cherie into his embrace, one arm under her legs, the other supporting her back. The breath whooshed out of her in a gasp of surprise. Her hands clutched his shoulders. Cherie was tall and she was all woman, an overflowing armful of warm flesh. He'd bet anything not many men would try to carry her like this. He, on the other hand, barely noticed the weight. Those workouts sure paid off when he wanted to sweep a woman off her feet.

He stepped in front of the backdrop, where he braced his legs apart in a heroic stance and bent over her. She stared up at him, her pupils widening until her eyes were storm-cloud gray. He knew this look. He'd seen it many times, in the throes of arousal. It meant she wanted him. It meant if they weren't in the middle of a crowded charity event, they'd be on each other in a millisecond.

That look made hope pound feverishly through his veins. She still wanted him, no matter what she said.

He leaned his head close to hers, so mere fractions of an inch separated them. At this distance, he saw the tiny pulse that beat at her temple, the glimmers of moss green in her irises, the dimple by her chin, the hint of sunburn at the peak of her cheekbones. He felt her heart rate skitter, her body tremble. Deep satisfaction settled in his gut. No doubt about it. She felt the pull just as much as he did. She might try to hide it or deny it or laugh it off or any of the other wacky things she'd done since they'd met. But he knew their crazy chemistry worked both ways.

Mutual knowledge hummed between them. Both were attracted; both were aware the other was attracted.

Cherie splayed her hand on his chest, as if to push him off. But the hell if he'd let her. He was tired of that inevitable arm's length she kept putting between them. She'd come here, into his territory, and she could damn well deal with the consequences. He tightened his grip.

"What are you doing?" she whispered fiercely.

"Giving you your money's worth," he growled. "Now smile for the camera."

She started to look toward the camera, but he shifted her so she was angled his direction. "For the camera, not at it. Look at me. I'm the one rescuing you from certain death."

She regained a bit of her usual bravado. "Certain death? My, my. That does sound dire."

"Oh, it is. You see, we were making love in the third floor bedroom. We were a little distracted." He adjusted his grip so one of his hands cradled her head. He knew how much she loved his hands.

"Let me guess. Things got so hot there was a spontaneous combustion."

"As soon as I saw the flames, I leaped into action."

"And put a helmet on me?"

"Sure. And some clothes. That part was a mistake." He let his eyes rake down her body and caught her shiver.

She swatted him on the chest, exactly how the other girl had, but with completely different results. Under his padded firefighter's pants, he went rock-hard and aching. If only they were alone, if only he could turn this little scene into something real, something that involved nothing but their two naked bodies and lots of moaning.

He bent his forehead to hers, fighting to get a grip on his hot need for her. "What is it? Why do you keep running away from me? It's like you're afraid of something."

"I'm not—"

"Are you afraid of someone?"

"Of course not," she said quickly.

Her right eyelid twitched.

The camera clicked.

"Awesome shot," said Fred. "We should put this one in the calendar."

"No," said Cherie quickly. "It's strictly personal." Her eyelid twitched again.

Vader knew he was on to something. Cherie was afraid . . . of something or someone.

As Vader let her slip back to her feet, he decided that one way or another, he was going to get the truth out of Cherie Harper. Once a man had been turned down twice, he deserved some answers. It was time to haul himself out of his funk and take some action.

He was damn tired of being underestimated.

About the Author

JENNIFER BERNARD is a graduate of Harvard and a former news promo producer. The child of academics, she confounded her family by preferring romance novels to . . . well, any other books. She left big-city life for true love in Alaska, where she now lives with her husband and stepdaughter. She's no stranger to book success, as she also writes erotic novellas under a naughty secret name not to be mentioned at family gatherings.

Visit her on the Web at www.JenniferBernard.net.

Visit www.AuthorTracker.com for exclusive information on your favorite HarperCollins authors.

About the Author

Give in to your impulses . . .
Read on for a sneak peek at six brand-new
e-book original tales of romance
from Avon Books.
Available now wherever e-books are sold.

ONCE UPON A HIGHLAND SUMMER
By Lecia Cornwall

HARD TARGET
By Kay Thomas

THE WEDDING DATE
A Christmas Novella
By Cara Connelly

TORN
A Billionaire Bachelors Club Novel
By Monica Murphy

THE CUPCAKE DIARIES: SPOONFUL OF CHRISTMAS
By Darlene Panzera

RODEO QUEEN
By T. J. Kline

An Excerpt from

ONCE UPON A HIGHLAND SUMMER

by Lecia Cornwall

An ancient curse, a pair of meddlesome
ghosts, a girl on the run, and a fateful
misunderstanding make for the perfect chance
at true love in Lecia Cornwall's latest novella.

"I'll have your decision now, if you please."

Lady Caroline Forrester stared at the carpet in her half-brother's study. It was like everything else in his London mansion—expensive, elegant, and chosen solely to proclaim his consequence as the Earl of Somerson. She fixed her eyes on the blue swirls and arabesques knotted into the rug and wondered what distant land it came from, and if she could go there herself rather than make the choice Somerson demanded.

"Come now," he said impatiently. "You have two suitors to choose from. Viscount Speed has two thousand pounds a year, and will inherit his father's earldom."

"In Ireland," Caroline whispered under her breath. Speed also had oily, perpetually damp skin and a lisp, and was only interested in her because her dowry would make him rich. At least for a short while, until he spent her money as he'd spent his own fortune—on mistresses, whist, and horses.

"And Lord Mandeville has a fine estate on the border with Wales. His mother lives there, so she would be company for you."

Mandeville spent no time at all in his country estate for that exact reason. Caroline had been in London only a month, but she'd heard the gossip. Lady Mandeville went through highborn companions the way Charlotte—Somerson's countess—devoured cream cakes at tea.

Lady Mandeville was famous for her bad temper, her sharp tongue, and her dogs. She raised dozens, perhaps even hundreds, of yappy, snappy, unpleasant little creatures that behaved just like their mistress, if the whispered stories were to be believed. The lady unfortunate enough to become Lord Mandeville's wife would serve as the old woman's companion until one of them died, with no possibility of quitting the post to take a more pleasant job.

"So which gentleman will you have?" Somerson demanded, pacing the room, his posture stiff, his hands clasped behind his back, his face sober. Caroline had laughed when he'd first told her the two men had offered for her hand. But it wasn't a joke. Her half-brother truly expected her to pick one of the odious suitors he'd selected for her and tie herself to that man for life. He looked down his hooked nose at her, a trait inherited from their father, along with his pale, bulging eyes. Caroline resembled her mother, the late earl's second wife, which was probably why Somerson couldn't stand the sight of her. As a young man he'd objected to his father's new bride most strenuously, because she was too young, too pretty, and the daughter of a mere baronet, without fortune or high connections. He'd even objected to the new countess's red hair. Caroline raised a hand to smooth a wayward russet curl behind her ear. Speed had red hair—orange, really—and spindly pinkish eyelashes.

Caroline thought of her niece Lottie, who was upstairs

having her wedding dress fitted, arguing with her mother over what shade of ribbon would best suit the flowers in the bouquet. She was marrying William Rutherford, Viscount Mears—*Caroline's* William, the man she'd known all her life, the eldest son and heir of the Earl of Halliwell, a neighbor and dear friend of her parents'. It had always been expected that she'd wed one of Halliwell's sons, but Sinjon, the earl's younger son, had left home to join the army and go to war rather than propose to Caroline. And now William, who even Caroline thought would make an offer for her hand, had instead chosen Lottie's hand. Caroline shut her eyes. It was beginning to feel like a curse. Not that it mattered now. William had made his choice. Still, a wedding should be a happy thing, the bride as joyful as Lottie, the future ripe with the possibilities of love and happiness.

Caroline didn't even *like* her suitors—well, they weren't really *her* suitors. They were courting her dowry, and a connection to Somerson. They needed her money, but they didn't need her.

An Excerpt from

HARD TARGET
by Kay Thomas

Kay Thomas' thrilling Elite Ops series kicks off
with an unlikely hero and a mother determined
to save her child. When Anna Mercado's son is
kidnapped, Former DEA agent Leland Hollis
agrees to deliver the ransom into dangerous
territory south of the border. Getting the boy
out of a violent cartel region involves risking
everything. And for that, Leland will have
to convince Anna to do the scariest thing
of all . . . open her heart and trust him.

"Could you hand me my top, please?"

Leland bent down to retrieve Anna's shirt and turned away, staring at the floor in front of him to give her privacy. What the hell was he doing? At least he'd given the room a cursory inspection to rule out cameras or bugs before he'd practically screwed her against the bedroom wall.

What he'd really wanted to tell her, before they'd gotten sidetracked by the birth control issue, was the same thing he'd wanted to tell her last night: She didn't have to do him to get Zach back. Whether or not they had sex had no bearing on whether he'd help find her son.

Not that he didn't want her. He did. So much so that his teeth ached.

He hadn't known her long, but what he knew fascinated him. To have dealt with everything she had in the past year and still be so strong—that inner strength captivated him.

It was important she not think he expected sex in exchange for his help. Sex wasn't some kind of payoff. He needed to clarify that right away.

Besides, neither of them was going to be able to sleep now. He sighed, zipped his cargo shorts, and pulled on his t-shirt and the shoulder holster with the Ruger. He shoved the larger

Glock into his backpack. This was going to be a long evening.

The night breeze had shifted the shabby curtain to the side, leaving an unobscured view into the room. He turned to face her, wondering if anyone on the street had just gotten an eyeful.

A red laser dot reflected off the wide shoulder strap of her tank top. Recognizing the threat, he dove for her, shouting, "Down. Get down!"

Leland tackled Anna around the waist and pulled her to the floor. A bullet hit the wall with a deceptively soft *sphlift*, right where she'd been standing half a second earlier.

He climbed on top of her, his heart rate skyrocketing, and covered her completely with his body. His boot was awkward. His knee came down between her legs, trapping her in the skirt. More shots slapped the stucco, but they were all hitting above his head.

The gunman must be using a silencer. A loud car engine revved in the street. Voices shouted, and bullets flew through the window, no longer silenced.

How many shooters were there?

A flaming bottle whooshed through the window. It broke on impact, and fire spread rapidly across the dry plywood floor. The pop of more bullets against the wall sounded deceptively benign.

"What's happening?" Anna's lips were at his ear.

Her warm breath would have felt seductive if not for the shots flying overhead and the fire licking at his ass. He was crushing her with his body weight, but it was the only way to protect her from the onslaught.

"Why are they shooting at us?" Her voice was thin, like she was having trouble breathing.

He propped himself up on his elbows to take his weight off of her chest but kept his head down next to hers. "They want the money."

"How do they know about the ransom?" she asked.

"Everyone within a hundred miles knows about it." He raised his head cautiously.

They were nose to nose, but he ignored the intimacy of the position. They had to get out of the smoke-filled room. In here, even with just half the money, they were sitting ducks.

He needed his bag. It held all his ammunition and the Glock 17. And they couldn't leave the cash, not now anyway. The money might be the only thing that could keep them alive when they got out of here.

"Come on." He rolled to the side and tugged Anna's hand to pull her along with him. "But don't raise your head."

Another bullet hit the wall where she had been moments before. God, how many men were there? Knowing that could make a difference in getting out of this alive.

An Excerpt from

THE WEDDING DATE
A Christmas Novella
by Cara Connelly

In this sexy holiday novella, rising star and
award-winning author Cara Connelly launches
a new series about the magic of weddings!

"Blind dates are for losers." Julie Marone pinched the phone with her shoulder and used both hands to scrape the papers on her desk into a tidy pile. "You really think I'm a loser?"

"Not a *loser*, exactly." Amelia's inflection kept her options open.

Julie snorted a laugh. "Gee, thanks, sis. Tell me how you *really* feel."

"You know what I mean. You've been out of circulation for three years. You have to start *somewhere*."

"Sure, but did it have to be at the bottom of the barrel?"

"Peter's a nice guy!" Amelia protested.

"Absolutely," Julie said agreeably. "So devoted to dear old mom that he *still lives in her basement*."

Amelia let out a here-we-go-again groan. "He's an optometrist, for crying out loud. I assumed he'd have his own place."

Julie started on the old saying about what happens when you *assume*, but Amelia cut her off. "Yeah, yeah. Ass. You. Me. Got it. Anyway, Leo"—tonight's date—"is a definite step up. I checked with his sister"—Amelia's hair stylist—"and she said he's got a house in Natick. His practice is thriving."

"So why's he going on a blind date?"

"His divorce just came through."

Julie groaned. Recently divorced men fell into two categories. "Shopping for a replacement or still simmering with resentment?"

"Come on, Jules, give him a chance."

Julie sighed, slid the stack of papers into a folder marked *Westin/Anderson*, and added it to her briefcase for tomorrow's closing. "Just tell me where to meet him."

"On Hanover Street at seven. He made reservations at a place on Prince."

"Well, in that case." Dinner in Boston's North End almost made it worthwhile. Julie was always up for good Italian. "How will I recognize him? Tall, dark, and handsome?" A girl could hope.

"Dark . . . but . . . not tall. Wearing a red scarf."

"Handsome?"

Amelia cleared her throat. "I caught one of his commercials the other night. He's got a nice smile."

"Whoa, wait. Commercials? What kind of lawyer is he?"

"Personal injury." Amelia dropped it like a turd. Then said, "Oh, look, Ray's here. Gotta go," and hung up.

"How did I get into this?" Julie murmured.

The catalyst, she knew, was Amelia's own upcoming Christmas Eve wedding. She wanted Julie—her maid of honor—to bring a date. A real date, not her gay friend Dan. Amelia loved Dan like a brother, but he was single too, always up for hanging out, and he made it too easy for Julie to duck the dating game.

So Amelia had lined up three eligible men and informed Julie that if she didn't give them a chance, then their mother—a confirmed cougar with not-great taste in men—would bring a wedding date for her.

Recognizing a train wreck when she saw one coming, Julie had given in and agreed to date all three. So far they were shaping up even worse than expected.

Jan appeared in the doorway. "J-Julie?" Her usually pale cheeks were pink. Her tiny bosom heaved. "Oh, Julie. You'll never believe . . . the most . . . I mean . . . ."

"Take a breath, Jan." Julie did that thing where she pointed two fingers at Jan's eyes, then back at her own. "Focus."

Jan sucked air through her nose, let it out with a wheeze. "Okay, we just had a walk-in. From Austin." She wheezed again. "He's *gorgeous*. And that drawl . . . ." Wheeze.

Julie nodded encouragingly. It never helped to rush Jan.

"He said . . ." Jan fanned herself, for real. She was actually perspiring. "He said someone in the ER told him about you."

That sounded ominous.

Julie glanced at her watch. Five forty-five, too late to deal with mysterious strangers. If she left now, she'd just have time to get home and change into something more casual for her date.

"Ask him to come back tomorrow," she said. "I don't have time—"

"He just wants a minute." Jan wiped her palms on her grey, pleated skirt. At twenty-five, she dressed like Julie's Gram, but inside she was stuck at sixteen, helpless in the face of a handsome man. "I-I'm sorry. I couldn't say no."

Julie blew out a sigh, wondering—again—why she'd hired

her silly cousin in the first place. Because family was family, that's why.

"Fine. Send him in."

Ten seconds later, six-foot-two of Texan filled her door. Tawny hair, caramel eyes, tanned cheekbones.

Whoa.

An Excerpt from

TORN
A Billionaire Bachelors Club Novel
by *Monica Murphy*

The boys of *New York Times* bestselling author
Monica Murphy's sexy Billionaire Bachelors
Club are back, and this time, they're mixing
business with pleasure. Poised to snatch up
Marina Knight's real estate empire, sexy tycoon
Gage Emerson is on the verge of making an enemy
for life—even if he can make her melt with a single
kiss! But when Gage discovers that this alluring
creature is the key to his latest acquisition, he
must get to know the fierce woman willing to face
him down—as she steadily steals his heart.

"This is a huge mistake."

"What is?" He settles those big hands of his on my waist. His long fingers span outward, gripping me tight, and I feel like I've been seized by some uncontrollable force, one I can't fight off no matter how hard I try.

That force would be Gage.

"I already told you." God, he's exasperating. It's like he doesn't even listen to a word I say. "Us. Together. There will never be an 'us' or a 'together,' got it?"

"Got it, boss." He's not really listening, I can tell. He's pulled away slightly so that he can stare down at me, enraptured by the sight of his hands on my body. A shock of brown hair tinged with gold tumbles down across his forehead, and I resist the urge to reach out and push it away from his face.

Just barely.

He slides his hands around me until they settle at the small of my back, his fingertips barely grazing my backside. I'm wearing jeans, yet it's like I can feel his touch directly on my skin. Heat rushes over me, making my head spin, and I let go of a shaky exhalation.

"We shouldn't do this," I whisper, pressing my lips together when I feel his hands slide over my butt. Oh my God, his touch feels so good.

What the hell am I *thinking*, letting him touch me like this? It's wrong. Us together is wrong.

So why does it feel so right?

"Do what?" His question sounds innocent enough, but his touch isn't. He pulls me into him so that I can feel the unmistakable ridge of his erection pressing against my belly, and a gasp escapes me. He's big. Thick. My thighs shake at the thought of him entering me.

I need to put a stop to this, and quick.

"I don't think we sh—"

Gage presses his index finger to my lips, silencing me. I stare up at him, entranced by the glow in his eyes, the way he stares at my mouth. Like he's a starving man dying to devour me.

Anticipation thrums through my veins. I should walk away now. Right now, before we take this any further. We're standing in the doorway of the bakery for God's sake. Anyone could see us, not that many people are roaming the downtown sidewalks at this time of night. He's got one hand sprawled across my ass, and he's tracing my lips with his finger like he wants to memorize the shape of them.

And I'm . . . parting my lips so I can suck on his fingertip.

His eyes darken as he slips his finger deeper into my mouth. I close my lips around him, sucking, tasting his salty skin with a flick of my tongue. A rough, masculine sound rumbles from his chest as his hand falls away from my lips. He drifts his fingers down my chin, then my neck, and my breath catches in my throat.

"Gage." I whisper his name, confused. Is it a plea for him to stop or for him to continue? I don't know. I don't know what I want from him.

"Scared?" he asks, his lids lifting so that he can pin me with his gorgeous green eyes. They're glittering in the semi-darkness, full of so much hunger, and my body responds, pulsating with need.

I try my best to offer a snide response, but the truth comes out instead: "Terrified."

He lowers his head. I can feel his breath feather across my lips, and I part them in anticipation, eager for his kiss. "That makes two of us," he whispers.

Just before he settles his mouth on mine.

An Excerpt from

THE CUPCAKE DIARIES:
SPOONFUL OF CHRISTMAS

by Darlene Panzera

For fans of Debbie Macomber comes a special
holiday-themed installment of Darlene Panzera's
popular Cupcake Diaries series.

Andi glanced at the number on the caller ID, picked up the phone, and tried to mimic the deep, sultry voice of a sexy siren. "Hello, Creative Cupcakes."

"What if I told you I'd like to order a Mistletoe Magic cupcake with a dozen delicious kisses on top?"

She smiled at the sound of Jake's voice. "Mistletoe Magic?"

"I was guaranteed that the person who eats it will receive a dozen kisses by midnight."

"What if I told you," Andi said, playing along, "that you don't have to eat a cupcake to get a kiss and the magic will begin the minute you walk through the front door?"

Jake chuckled. "I'm on my way."

Andi's sister Kim and best friend Rachel watched her with amused expressions on their faces.

"I hope Mike and I still flirt with each other after *we're* married," Rachel said, her singsong voice a tease. "But the name Mistletoe Magic isn't half bad. Maybe we *should* make a red velvet cupcake with a Hershey's Kiss and miniature holly leaf sprinkles on top."

Kim finished boxing a dozen Maraschino cherry cupcakes and handed them to the customer at the counter. "As if we don't have enough sales already."

"Sales are great," Andi agreed. "We've booked orders for eighteen holiday parties. Now if I could only figure out what to get Jake for Christmas, life would be perfect."

Rachel rang up the next customer's order. "Mike and I decided our Hollywood honeymoon will be our gift to each other."

"Are you serious?" Kim picked up a pastry bag from the back worktable. "You—the woman who can't walk three feet past a store window without buying anything—are not going to get Mike a Christmas gift? Not even a little something?"

"It *is* hard," Rachel admitted. "But I promised him I wouldn't. I also promised I wouldn't go overboard with spending on the wedding arrangements."

"You could always have a small, simple wedding like Jake and I did," Andi suggested.

Rachel's red curls bounced back and forth as she shook her head. "I already booked the Liberty Theater for the reception. I know it's expensive, but the palace-like antique architecture was so beautiful I couldn't help myself. I've always dreamed of—"

"Being Cinderella?" Kim joked.

"I *do* want a Cinderella wedding," Rachel crooned. "I figure I can bake my own cake and skimp on other wedding details to stay within our budget."

Andi didn't think Rachel knew the first thing about staying within a budget but decided it was best not to argue. Instead she turned toward her younger sister. "Kim, what are you getting Nathaniel for Christmas?"

"I'm not sure." Kim averted her gaze. "Maybe I should just get him a new set of luggage tags."

Rachel frowned. "That's not very romantic."

"No, but it's practical," Andi said, coming to Kim's defense. "Nathaniel's probably getting her the same thing."

"He planned to fly to his family's home in Sweden this Christmas," Kim confessed, her dark brows drawing together. "But I told him I couldn't go, and he didn't want to go without me."

"Of course you can't go!" Rachel exclaimed, bracing her hands against the marble counter. "I need you to be my bridesmaid!"

"It would have been awkward spending Christmas with his family anyway," Kim said, piping vanilla icing over the cupcakes. "It's not like I'm part of his family, or like we're even engaged. In fact, I don't know what we are."

"You two are great together," Andi encouraged. "You both are artistic, enjoy nature, and love to travel."

Kim nodded, then looked up, her expression earnest. "But what *else*? I'm beginning to wonder if I should tell Nathaniel to go to Sweden without me."

"And miss my wedding? But you'll need a dance partner at the reception," Rachel reminded her. "He wouldn't go and leave you stranded without a date on Christmas Eve, would he?"

Kim hesitated. "I don't know."

The bells on the front door jingled as a man in his late forties entered the shop with a briefcase in hand.

"Are you the owners of Creative Cupcakes?" he asked, looking hopeful.

Andi stepped forward and smiled. "Yes, we are."

The man placed his briefcase at the end of the counter and sprung the latch. "Then I have an offer I think you might like."

"What kind of offer?" Rachel asked, anticipation lighting her faintly freckled face.

The man handed them each a set of papers a half-inch thick. "An offer to buy Creative Cupcakes."

An Excerpt from

RODEO QUEEN
by T. J. Kline

Sydney Thomas wants nothing more than to train
rodeo horses and hopes becoming a rodeo queen
will help her make the contacts she seeks. She
is thrilled when Mike Findley hires her for her
dream job as a horse trainer . . . until she meets
Scott Chandler, the other half of Findley Brothers
stock contractors. He's arrogant, judgmental,
and, unfortunately, unbelievably sexy.

Scott gave her a rakish, lopsided grin. "Oh, that's right. You can outride me." His brow arched as he articulated her words back to her. "Any day of the week."

It took everything in her to try to ignore how good looking this infuriating man was. He towered over her—well over six feet tall—and the black cowboy hat that topped a mop of dark brown hair, barely curling at his collar, gave him a devilish appearance. With sensuous lips and a square jaw, his deeply tanned face reflected raw male sexuality. She wasn't sure if he was actually as muscular as his broad shoulders seemed to indicate due to his unruly western shirt, but his jeans left no imagining necessary when it came to his sculpted thighs. And his jet black eyes almost unnerved her. Those eyes were so dark that Sydney felt she would drown if she continued to meet his gaze.

So much for ignoring his good looks, she chided herself. "Give me a chance out there today to prove it."

"I don't see why she can't run them, Scott." Jake must have decided that it was time to break up the showdown with his two cents. "She is certainly experienced enough, more than most of the girls you let run flags."

Scott glared at Jake before turning back to Sydney. She

caught Jake's conspiratorial wink and decided that she liked this old cowboy. Scott would be hard pressed to find a reason to deny her request now that Jake had sold him out.

"Fine, you can do both. But, if anything goes wrong, if a steer so much as takes too long in the arena, you're finished. Got it, Miss Thomas?" The warning note in his voice was unmistakable.

Sydney flashed a dazzling smile. "Call me Sydney, and it's no problem." She clutched her shoulder. "Unless I'm unable to hold the flags because someone ran me into a fencepost."

His look told her he didn't appreciate her sense of humor. "I mean it. Rodeo starts at 10 sharp. Be down here at 9:30, ready to go."

As the sassy cowgirl walked away, Scott shook his head. "What in the world possessed you to open your mouth, Jake?"

"Aw, Scott, she'll do fine. Besides, you did run her down with Wiley at the gate. You kinda owed her one."

Scott watched Sydney head for the gate, taking in her small waist, the spread of her hips in her red pants, and her lean, denim-encased legs. That woman was all curves, moving with the grace of a jungle cat. With her full, pouting lips and those golden eyes, it certainly wouldn't be painful to look at her all day. "I guess."

Scott mounted Wiley and headed to change into his clean shirt and show chaps but couldn't seem to shake the image of Sydney Thomas from his mind. He knew that she'd been attracted to him—he'd seen it in her blush—but he'd had enough run-ins with ostentatious rodeo queens over the years, including his ex-fiancée, to know that they simply wanted to tame a cowboy. It was doubtful that this one was any different, although she did have a much shorter temper than most. He chuckled as he recalled how the gold in her eyes seemed to spark when she was irritated. He wondered if her eyes flamed up whenever she was passionate. Scott shook his head to clear it of visions of the sexy spitfire. No time for that. He had a rodeo to get started.